QUILTERS OF THE BUNCO CLUB:
Phree & Rosa

Book 2 of The Bunco Club Series

Also by Karen DeWitt

The Bunco Club

Quilters of The Bunco Club: Phree & Rosa

Cover by Karen DeWitt.

Published by Frame Masters, Ltd.
Matteson, Il 60443

ISBN-13: 978-0615992051
ISBN-10: 0615992056

Printed in the United States of America.

QUILTERS OF THE BUNCO CLUB:
Phree & Rosa

Book 2 of The Bunco Club Series

Karen DeWitt

To Lois -
Happy Quilting! -
Karen DeWitt

Frame Masters, Ltd.
Matteson, Illinois 60443

To Rob: my boy, my joy

List of Bunco Club Characters

Phreedom (Phree) Clarke: Divorced (Gary, aka The Bastard), mother of Emily, discovered valuable Mayflower documents, quilter

Rosa Mitchell: Married (Terry), mother of Ricky and Alex, quilter, owns The Pizza Depot with her husband

Lettie Peabody: Fiber artist, single woman, quilter

Nedra Lange: Widow (John), mother of two college age daughters, Executive Assistant to Editor-in-Chief at *Excel* Magazine, quilter

Marge Russell: Married (Bud), three children, nurse, quilter, control freak

Helen Delaney: Married (Ben), mother of two, works at Quilter's Closet, quilter and long-arm quilter

Beth Stevenson: Married (Tim), mother of three, salon owner/stylist, quilter, hoarder

Nancy Walsh: Single /Boyfriend (Michael), learning disabilities tutor, quilter

Sunnie Eaton: Phree's mother

Brian Barber: Brother of Nedra Lange, lawyer

Chapter 1
Early Spring - Phree

"I'll take it," Phree told the stunned realtor who looked at her with a cross of disbelief and something akin to the stinkeye.

"Are you saying that you want to buy this property and for...uh, what did you call it, a quilting retreat?"

"Please stop looking at me like I'm crazy, Sue. And yes, I want this. I've dreamed about owning these buildings since the last nun moved out of this convent, and the For Sale sign was posted when my daughter was only six years old."

"Didn't you say Emily is starting college this fall? That's gotta be close to, what—twelve years?"

"Exactly, and that's why I don't want to wait another minute." The hinges of the heavy wooden door complained with several high-pitched squeals as the realtor tugged it closed. "What happens next? Do we sign papers? Do I put down earnest money? I'd like to take possession as soon as possible."

The former convent was located south of Chicago, in the community of Whitney. Its footprint was planted firmly in suburbia, while its 'toes' danced in the beginnings of rural Illinois. Along with an ever-growing population, a handful of farms called Whitney home, and the diversity added to the well-rounded community. Farm after farm of corn or soybeans began their western and southward journey through the state at the outskirts of Whitney. Sauk Trail Creek ran through the town, and just before the countryside opened up to endless flatlands, dense woods edged the creek on both sides. This had been a peaceful and isolated location 62 years ago when the Carmelite Order constructed a sprawling convent in the Midwest to house a community of nuns.

A consolidation in the mid-'90s relocated the remaining Sisters from their Chicagoland home to various convents and monasteries around the country. Years of red tape were eventually sorted out, and the property went up for sale. For a while Whitney was abuzz with rumors: an unnamed rapper was interested, a religious cult wanted to buy the complex, even Hugh Hefner was reported to have made a clandestine visit while shopping for a new Bunny Hutch. No offers had ever materialized, and after years had gone by, the locals essentially forgot the empty and well-hidden convent was even there—except for Phree Clarke.

Jiggling the knob to make sure it had locked properly, the realtor turned to Phree with hopeful eyes. "After all this time on the market, I'm sure the sellers will be agreeable to a quick sale."

Phree had lowballed an offer to get things started, and if it were accepted, she would have secured one heck of a deal. The two women walked past the sprawling brick building and down a long sidewalk toward the parking lot where their cars were parked side by side. Even though shrinking mounds of melting snow dotted the property, tenacious spikes of grass and weeds poked from ancient cracks in the pavement.

"Have you been preapproved for a mortgage yet?"

"To tell the truth, I plan on paying with cash." Phree felt the heady rush of achieving a longtime goal, as giddiness threatened to bubble out of her being.

The realtor stopped walking, and her eyebrows shot up so high under her bangs that Phree could no longer see them. "Cash?"

"Yeah, that dirty, smelly, green stuff." Phree rubbed her fingers together for effect.

"Um…okay. Would you be able to stop by my office later this afternoon and sign papers so we can get the ball rolling?" Eager to please, Sue added, "Or if it's more convenient, I could come by your home."

As the two women shook hands, Phree wished she could be there when this newbie realtor told her boss that her very first client had just bought the old convent that had been on the market for nearly twelve years.

"You go ahead. I'm going to hang back for a while and study the structure some more."

"I can walk you through the building again if you're having doubts." Sue sounded worried, and Phree figured that in this short amount of time the nervous young woman had mentally spent a good portion of her first commission.

Phree shaded her eyes and watched as early spring warblers flitted between leafless trees, trilling their cheery songs. "No worries, Sue. I'm definitely buying this place. I just want to enjoy the dream a little longer."

Many months ago, while rummaging through an old trunk left behind after her grandmother passed away, Phree had discovered a bounty of hidden historical artifacts from her Mayflower ancestors. A flurry of publicity followed, and when it was all over, Phreedom Aquarius Eaton Clarke was a very, *very* wealthy woman.

The dream that had lived in her heart for decades, unintentionally placed there by her quilting mother and her embroidery loving great-grandmother, was to one day own a quilting retreat. Her plan would focus on a community where women with a love for any type of needlework or fiber art could be creative, share ideas, and network with each other.

Because of Phree's ancestors, she was about to own a nearly forgotten, once thriving convent nestled in a wooded rural setting that had formerly housed several dozen nuns. She decided to honor the sturdy, fearless people in her lineage by naming her quilting community The Mayflower Quilters Retreat.

As she slid into her car and took a final look at the building, a nagging thought played with the edges of Phree's mind: would any of her seven close friends from the Bunco Club be envious? Would owning a quilters retreat cause a fissure to grow in their friendship until it could never be spanned? Phree thought not—she fiercely hoped not...because at this point nothing could stop her from moving forward.

Chapter 2
The Bunco Club's Long Awaited Las Vegas Trip

"This is an absolutely perfect way to end our trip, but I have one question," Nancy said as she placed a claret colored linen napkin in her lap. "Do we *have* to go home tomorrow morning? Can't we all stay here forever, pleeeease?"

"The days went by way too fast," Phree said, "but I'm so glad that we could all share such a fun escape." Phree had planned this trip for months. She couldn't think of a better way to celebrate her remarkable discovery of Mayflower antiquities than spending several days in Las Vegas with her best friends from the Bunco Club. While the difficulty of eight women rearranging schedules had made for some tension-filled pre-Vegas moments, all stress evaporated with take-off from Midway Airport in Chicago.

Now, three days later, the friends were seated at the premiere window table in the Eiffel Tower Restaurant of the Paris Hotel and Casino. Flawless red roses stood soldier straight in a crystal vase that dazzled as though made of diamonds. Below them the Las Vegas Strip quivered with silent movement. The soft hum from the fine diners as they enjoyed each other's company over a gourmet meal had replaced the drone of street-level machinery and honking car horns. The occasional tinkling of ice in a sparkling goblet resonated throughout the room.

"I bet between the eight of us we've got at least a thousand pictures," Helen said. "I was thinking that we should combine our photos and make one of those digital books. Then we could each have a copy."

"Ooooh, what a great idea. I like that," Lettie said.

Phree accepted the menu from the server. "Let's start with some wine. Is everybody okay with that?" She looked toward Beth. "Would you prefer a soft drink or virgin daiquiri?"

"A virgin strawberry daiquiri sounds amazing."

The drinks arrived right after the dinner orders were taken, and Marge stood to make a toast. Extending her wineglass toward Phree, she said, "One final toast of thanks for the memories we have stitched together over the past few days. To Phree!"

The women chorused, "To Phree," and some added "Thank you" or "Here, here" at the end.

Phree nodded and smiled graciously as everyone took a sip from her glass. Not one of these women held any ill will or jealousy toward her for the windfall she experienced from the Mayflower discovery, and she felt certain they would revel in her ownership of a quilters retreat. They were happy for her; they were true friends. Resting her wineglass on the table she said, "We've stuffed so many activities into our four days and three nights, that it would be fun to share what everyone liked the best. I know this probably sounds lame, but I'd like to go around the table and hear everyone's favorite memory while we were in Vegas." She was happy when no one groaned over her suggestion. Instead the women smiled, as though they also thought this was a good idea. She looked to her left and said, "Let's start with Nancy."

"No fair, I don't want to go first. There were so many great things we did, that I need to think about this for a few minutes."

Beth waved her hand in the air; a delicate bracelet slipped down her arm. "I'll go first," she said. "I know exactly what my favorite moment was."

"When you won $53.00 on that video poker game, and you were so excited that you pushed your chair back so fast you knocked it over?" joked Nedra.

"Not exactly, but thanks for reminding everyone of that embarrassing moment, Ned. By the way, you forgot to mention that I almost took out a cocktail waitress with a full tray of drinks at the same time." Beth looked into Phree's eyes and said, "I can't tell you how great it was to walk into that hair salon and have someone who knew exactly what she was doing color, cut, and style my hair. I'm so used to throwing on some color when the salon is closed and hacking at my own hair in the mirror. Do you know how hard it is to cut your own hair and have it look semi-decent?"

"You always do a great job on our hair," Rosa said. "We all love what you do."

"But the pleasure of sitting in the beauty chair and talking with another professional was so much fun for me. On top of it, I *love* my new color and highlights, and I *really* love what she did with the angle of the cut. I guess there's no other way but to come back here every month to get my hair done." Beth smiled at Phree. "Best moment for me…a big girl salon experience."

Eager to share her favorite Vegas memory, Helen jumped in. "My best moment is similar to Beth's, but at the same time way different. I enjoyed our little afternoon tea at Bellagio's the most. The finger sandwiches and desserts were like eating little pieces of art. And not to sound too braggy, but it was great to eat scones that someone else made that are as good, if not better, than mine. I loved the elegant atmosphere with the pianist playing the baby grand—it was intimate, but at the same time we never lost sight of the fact that we were in Vegas." Looking at Beth she said, "When you come back here for your hair next month, I'll come with, and we can do afternoon tea again."

"As long as we're discussing Bellagio's," Lettie said, "I could put up a tent in the lobby and stare at that Chihuly glass ceiling forever. Talk about being inspired. When I get home I'm going right out to my studio to try to incorporate the colors and organic feel of that piece into my fiber art." Lettie chuckled, "And talk about pictures—I bet I have several hundred alone of that ceiling."

Phree was surprised when Rosa offered the next favorite without any coaxing. "My favorite thing was that I was able to forget about my son for a few minutes and have some fun for a change. While that makes me feel horribly guilty, it also makes me realize how much I've insulated myself from everything other than Ricky." Rosa pulled her shoulders into a shrug. "I have to thank Lettie for convincing me, or should I say nagging me, to come on this trip. If she hadn't stepped in, I would have stayed at home being miserable and afraid. A few days in Vegas with my seven good friends was just what I needed."

Phree knew that Lettie had browbeaten Rosa, as only a best friend can do, not only about coming to Vegas, but about the despair she was sinking into after her fourteen-year-old son had run away from home last December. "I think I finally reached her," Lettie had said. "We're going to have to be patient with Rosa and hope that Ricky shows up soon."

Nedra covered her face with her hands. "Okay, I suppose you all know what my best moment, or should I say moments were."

At the same time all seven women chorused, "Craps!"

She pulled her hands away from her face and said, "I forgot how much fun craps can be. John and I came to Vegas for our honeymoon and managed to get back here a few times after that. We'd have a ball at the craps table. After he died, I thought I'd never come back to this town and certainly never play craps again. But there I was, usually the last one to come up to our suite at night. I felt like I was keeping John's memory alive yet at the same time letting go. Does that make sense? Anyway, it felt good." Making eye contact with the two women who had yet to acknowledge their special moments, she said, "Who's next? Marge? Nancy?"

"I guess it's my time to surprise everyone a little," Marge, the Sarge, said.

"Do tell," Beth teased.

"My favorite memory would be our spa day."

"What!" three of the group said at once.

"We had to practically drag you kicking and screaming that day," Nancy said. "To paraphrase, I believe your words went something like this, 'I've never had a facial or massage or any of this fancy crap, and I really don't see any need to waste Phree's money on a spa day for me.' "

"So sue me," Marge laughed. "I've already decided I'm going for a massage once a month when I get home. Who knows, I might get a facial at the same time."

Rosa said, "Now I've heard everything."

The waitstaff scurried around the table picking up empty plates and utensils from the appetizers and salads.

"I guess I'm next," Nancy said. "It looks like the food will be here soon so I'll make this quick—just one word describes my best moments: shopping."

"Uh-oh, I think I created a monster," Nedra said.

"Yeah I think you did," Nancy told her. "Nedra and I did some shopping at the Fashion Mall and Caesar's, and I *loved* it. I love how it makes me feel to wear clothes that are made well and fit right, especially after losing so much weight. I had the most excellent fun that day, Ned, I'll never forget it."

Serving trays with artistically plated dinners were carried to their table and placed on tray stands.

"What about Phree?" Beth said. "You have to tell us your favorite moment."

Eleven floors down at street level the fountains at Bellagio silently danced their water ballet, as Phree said, "My best memories of this trip were all the happy moments we shared. The look of awe from those of you who were Vegas 'virgins' was priceless. It was better than I had hoped. I enjoyed the fun of being able to afford the most elegant accommodations for all of us along with our spa and salon days. But most of all, my best takeaway is the eight of us piecing together another block in the evolving journey of our friendship."

In the dim lighting and quiet of the limo, Phree relaxed into the plush leather seat. Amidst a final volley of hugs and thanks, the seven women had all been delivered safely back home. Everyone had enjoyed herself in Las Vegas, and during the drive from the airport the women had commented on how hard it would be to get back to reality.

"It seems like we've been gone for weeks and not just days. After all," Nancy sighed, "I suppose that's why they call it a vacation."

"I'm already missing the warm weather out there, and I haven't even gotten out of the car yet." Lettie held up the scarf and gloves that were nestled in her lap and shaking them said, "Back to these things for a while, I guess."

"It won't be long before it starts warming up," Marge said. "It's already the end of April—at least all of the snow has melted."

As the women adjusted to the truth that they, indeed, were back home in the Chicago suburbs and, in most cases, headed off to work tomorrow, Phree held close to one final secret. She wouldn't share the news of the retreat with her friends until she was notified that her offer on the convent had been accepted.

Chapter 3
Phree

"Okay ladies, it's my big moment, let's line up," Phree announced to her seven closest friends, all members of the Bunco Club. They nudged into position on the steps leading up to the old convent. Phree could envision comfortable wicker rocking chairs and two-seater porch swings scattered about the wraparound porch. During warm weather, women would be able to relax, chat, or do handwork in this peaceful outdoor environment.

Sue, the *extremely* happy realtor, had shown up with keys trailing pretty colorful ribbons for all of the buildings on the compound. She had volunteered to take photos of Phree with her friends. Handing Phree a single red rose, and enfolding her first and forever memorable client in a hug, she whispered, "Thank you for opening so many doors to me. I'll never forget your kindness."

"You're very welcome," Phree answered. "And don't ever forget that you deserve every bit of it."

The Bunco Club had also brought flowers for their dear friend, and of course, something to eat—a chocolate cake with buttercream frosting that displayed the wish, 'Congratulations Phree and Success to The Mayflower Quilters Retreat'.

Marge, the Sarge, instructed the lined-up women. "Shoulders back, chins up, and suck in those stomachs, girls." Everyone obeyed her order as arms slipped behind backs, heads tilted toward one another, and smiles sprung to their lips. With a crisp command, she said, "Okay, Sue, you may now take the photograph."

The camera clicked, and clicked, and kept clicking, as the eight friends posed, relaxed, and then laughed when they all realized that Sue was still shooting their photograph. Phree knew those would be her favorite photos—the ones where they were relaxed and unaware, while laughing with each other.

"Ready for the tour?" Phree said, and everyone inched closer to the door. With an unsteady hand, she inserted the key into the lock. Phree's vision of a quilters retreat would soon become a reality, and while she was eager to begin this exciting phase of her life, she was also frightened beyond belief.

"I can't wait to hear your plans and ideas," Nancy said. "This is going to be the coolest thing in the whole area for quilters. Heck, maybe even the whole country."

Nedra and Beth said at exactly the same time, "Maybe even the whole world!"

From the moment Phree had told the surprised realtor that she would purchase the property, it had only taken seven weeks to close the deal. Phree had quickly learned what a lot of cash could do to expedite a closing date. So on this warm day in May, the large double doors of the neglected convent unlocked with a loud clunk, and the eight friends stepped into a cavernous entryway. Noonday sun filtered through a kaleidoscope of hues from the rose window that hung above the doors, scattering colors across the opposite wall. Ecru marble floors veined with rusty ginger greeted them, along with a high-domed ceiling edged in gold leaf.

"Wow," said Helen, "Those nuns really knew how to decorate back then. This room is completely empty, and it's still beautiful."

Front and center as they entered were three arched alcoves. They were lit with recessed lighting and edged in glittering gold leaf, and at one time must have held large statues. Phree pointed to two of the oversized niches. "I'd like to display quilts in these that could act as samples for classes we're offering. The quilts can change to sync with scheduled courses. Don't you think a fresh flower arrangement in the middle one would be beautiful and welcoming as quilters entered for the first time?"

The tour continued with Phree pointing out her ideas and explaining her plans for the various rooms on the main floor.

"I want to name the rooms after people and things from the Mayflower. Maybe the large sewing room will be called something like the George Soule Gathering Room or even just George Soule. Other rooms could be The Compact, Hannah Brewster, Plymouth, Miles Standish—something like that. I haven't quite figured it out yet, but I'd like to develop the Mayflower theme as much as possible."

"That sounds like a cool idea," Lettie said, and several of the women nodded their heads in agreement.

Beth smoothed her palm across a wall. "This place is in decent shape for having been empty so long. I was afraid it would be run down and beat-up, or even worse, vandalized."

"I was worried about that, too," Rosa said.

"From what I can tell, and I'm just guessing here...or maybe I should say hoping, but a good portion of the work will be cosmetic. Of course there are some big issues that need to be addressed—the biggest will be updating the kitchen. I *think* the structure itself is sound and was probably built to last a long time. And even though the building is somewhat old, they didn't seem to skimp on materials."

"I'd have to agree with that," Nancy said. "While it's sparse, it appears to be very well built."

"The caretakers lived in the house out back for eight years after the convent was empty. I assume the Carmelite Order didn't think it would take so long to sell the property, and they wanted to keep the buildings safe, especially from vandals. Eventually, when they removed all of the religious items, there was no longer any need for a caretaker." The women were standing in the spacious dining room, and Phree tapped a finger on one of four long wooden-planked tabletops. "I plan on using or repurposing as much of the old furnishings as possible. Like these fabulous dining tables. Aren't they beautiful?"

"There's not one thing in here that isn't beautiful," Nedra said.

"Where's the sewing area going to be?" asked Nancy.

"Right over here, ladies."

The women's footsteps echoed in the emptiness as Phree led the group to a set of double pocket doors. Sliding open the doors she revealed an expansive room boasting dark wood floors with a massive white-marble fireplace centered at one end. "This must have been a meeting room or community area of some sort." Phree continued the tour of the empty room, pointing to areas where she envisioned worktables, ironing boards, and other stations that would be necessary to a state-of-the-art quilters retreat. "I want to put some kind of mini-kitchen area over here. Just big enough for a microwave, a couple of coffee and tea makers, a small sink, and a little serving bar or table for treats."

"I can tell you've given this a lot of thought," Helen said. "It sounds wonderful."

"I've got a ton of ideas, and it's really exciting to have the pocketbook to make them happen." Phree leaned against the doorjamb and tucked her hands into the front pockets of her jeans. "There were times when this dream was all that stood between me and serious depression. I'm embarrassed to admit this, but through the years, especially when my ex was being his typical asshole self, I would sit in the parking lot and plan the whole quilters retreat in my head. I'd peek in the windows that weren't too high off the ground to get a feel for what was inside. I've loved this building since the first time I saw it." She pushed off from the decorative molding around the door with her shoulder as she said, "Come on, I'm dying to show you the rooms upstairs where the quilters will sleep. It's just too perfect.

"There are actually two ways to get upstairs. There's the big staircase by the front entry and a smaller set of service stairs by the back near the kitchen. I plan on turning one of them into an elevator to make sure the building is accessible to all quilters. It will also make it easier for everyone to schlep their week's worth of belongings up to the second floor." Turning to Marge she said, "I contacted your hubby to rewire all of the electricity for me. I want to have plenty of outlets for sewing machines and irons, and I don't want to have problems with fuses. All the workers start tomorrow."

"Bud's really excited about the project," Marge told her. "Renovating is his favorite kind of work. He likes to help people achieve the image they have in their head, and offer creative ideas for lighting and other electrical needs."

When they reached the top of the stairs Phree said, "Here's the sleeping area. There are twenty-four identical bedrooms, twelve on each side of the building. Each room is big enough to accommodate two twin beds and side-by-side rooms are connected by a large bathroom that the four quilters will share. That makes a maximum of forty-eight quilters if all of these rooms are full. Of course, there will be some women that might prefer a room to themselves."

"Why would anyone want to do that?" asked Beth.

"I suspect health concerns would be the number one reason, then possibly snoring, or an extremely light sleeper, or even just personality issues. Of course there will have to be an increased charge for a single."

The women snaked their way through several of the rooms commenting about various things as they went, and Phree directed them to the end of the hallway. "This is one of the suites. They must have been for the head nuns or whatever they're called—or maybe reserved for important visiting nuns and guests, or even family members." She opened the door for her friends to enter. "There are four identical suites—two at each end of the hallway. I thought these would be great for our instructors and guest speakers."

"Holy cow!" Beth said. "This verges on luxurious!" The women oohed and aahed their way through the suite and private bath.

"It's like an oversized one-bedroom apartment on steroids," Nedra said, "with an incredible view."

The eight friends gathered at the expansive windows that overlooked the compound. Phree pointed. "That's the caretaker's house where I'll live." Beyond the caretaker's home was a solid wall of trees, newly leafed out in the late spring sun. Phree spotted what might be an overgrown path. It would stand to reason that the Sisters who had lived here might have enjoyed a reflective walk in the woods on occasion. She'd have to check it out, and if the path showed promise, add it to the growing list of chores the landscapers would need to address.

There was still much more to show her friends, but she turned to them and said, "I know some of you have to get back to work, but I want each of you to know how much I appreciate that you were here to share this moment with me. It means a lot that I wasn't alone when I put that key in the door for the first time."

"I'm sure Emily would have been here if she wasn't in school." Marge patted Phree's back.

"I know she would have," Phree said. "She's very excited for me…for us. But with only a few weeks left of high school, she didn't need to take time off for this. Besides, she did several walk-throughs with the realtor and me while we were waiting for the sale to go through."

"Does your mom know about the retreat?" Helen asked.

Phree blew a sharp puff of air from her nose, and at the same time she said, "Hmmph. I e-mailed Sunnie, but she never responded. Typical, I'd say. I thought with Wolf being gone she might show some interest in their only child. Knowing Sunnie, she's probably involved in something she deems *more important* than supporting her daughter."

Rosa said, "Well, honey, it's her loss and our gain."

"And, as you guys like to call him, Officer Hottie will be stopping by after his shift is over today to share in the excitement."

Marge wrapped her knuckles on the wall, and all eyes turned her way. With her trademark authoritative voice she said, "Ladies, let's move along smartly and go downstairs. I think it's time we sit at one of those big, long tables and break it in Bunco-style—with a little chocolate cake and some nice white wine."

Chapter 4
Rosa

Looking in her rearview mirror, Rosa watched as Phree shielded her eyes from the bright sun. She waved to each driver as, one by one, the women pulled away from the parking lot and drove down the meandering lane toward the main road. Phree had asked if they could all gather again in a few days to act as a sounding board to her ideas for the retreat. She wanted to pick their brains about any thoughts or ideas they might have that could be helpful. Without fail, each woman had said she would be happy to help, and Rosa had felt a little trapped as she agreed to join the brainstorming session.

Rosa's youngest son, fourteen-year-old Ricardo (Ricky), also known as Cardo by the boys in juvie, had been missing for nearly six months. He had run away in December after stealing money, credit cards, and electronics at a Christmas Bunco, which included the players' family members, held at Marge's home. At first Rosa had been humiliated, assuming he would show up within a day or two with some belligerent, half-baked excuse for his behavior. When that didn't happen, she had gone into panic mode, which quickly led her down a path of intense hopelessness. What had she done wrong? What could she have done differently? Why was he doing this? Where could he be? All boiling down to the most terrifying question of all—Is my child still alive?

Her Bunco friends had been patient and understanding with her depression, trying to cheer her, including her in one-on-one activities, and sometimes just sitting with her for hours, or letting her cry until she could cry no more. Filled with fear, she had become paralyzed by panic and self-loathing as she went through long days powerless to do anything productive.

In early April, before the scheduled Las Vegas trip, Lettie, her closest friend, knocked on her door unannounced. Rosa remembered thinking, "Not again. Please just leave me alone." She was toying with not answering the door, but Lettie knew she rarely left the house anymore, and Lettie could be persistent.

"Get out of that robe and get some clothes on. I need your help with something."

Rosa stormed to the nearest chair and flounced onto the seat, robe billowing, sash and dust motes flying. "Come on, I'm not stupid," she argued. "This is just a ploy to get me out of the house, and try to put a smile on my face." If she was mean enough, even Lettie might give up and leave.

"And if it is, so what?" Lettie looked over the remnants of an unattended home, and Rosa could read disgust in her eyes. It had been weeks, maybe months, since she had made an attempt at house cleaning. Carryout boxes and bags, mostly from the restaurant that Rosa co-owned with her husband, littered the room along with paper plates, coffee mugs, newspapers, and unopened mail. "I'm sick of you moping around all day being pissed off and scared." Arcing her arm over the messy living room, she said, "Look at this place." And softening her tone added, "This isn't you, Rosa."

"I didn't ask for you or anyone else to give a shit. Why don't you just go away and leave me alone?" Pausing for a beat, she then spit out, "Find somebody else who wants a pretend mother." Rosa was being just plain cruel. She hoped the impact of her last comment would cause Lettie to turn on her heel, run out the door, and never look back. In her early fifties, Lettie was single and childless, and years ago had confided in Rosa that her biggest regret in life was not being a mother.

Rosa watched as her friend recoiled from the nasty barb. She had hit her mark, but to her credit, she felt a twinge of shame. Rather than bolt from the room, Lettie made smoldering eye contact with her friend, bent at the waist, and got in Rosa's face. "Be as mean and spiteful as you want, girl, but I'm not going to let you wallow in this mess anymore. You're coming with me today."

Another ten or fifteen minutes of arguing and accusations went by while Rosa reluctantly got herself presentable enough to leave the house. It climaxed when they got in Lettie's truck. Her dearest friend said, "Don't you think that your husband is just as devastated as you are? Yet Terry goes to work every day keeping the doors to The Pizza Depot open. The business, I might remind you, that the two of you built from nothing and that still needs your input."

Lettie gripped the steering wheel so tightly that her knuckles paled, and Rosa could tell her friend was trying to maintain a semblance of control.

"And what about Ricky? What if he came home today, Rosa? Look at you. Look what he'd find. He wouldn't find his mother, the woman he needed. He wouldn't even find the structured home life that he left. He'd find a woman that can't even comb her hair in the morning. A woman who couldn't handle whatever he might need if he showed up looking for the loving family he left behind."

Lettie eased her tone a little. "I know you think everything will be okay once he comes home, but you've got to realize he's going to need a lot of help and stability when that happens." Lettie took her friend's too thin hand in hers as she said, "He'll need you to be strong. He's going to need his mother waiting with hugs and support when he comes home. He'll expect to have everything exactly like it was when he left." Putting the vehicle in gear, she eased her foot onto the gas pedal, and started driving before saying, "We're going to take the first steps to finding Rosa today. You have to be prepared for Ricky's sake when he returns."

Bitterness and anger engulfed Rosa as she silently sat in Lettie's truck trying to figure out where they were going. How had she allowed herself to be bamboozled into this little field trip? The familiar surroundings gave her no clue to their undisclosed destination; it could be anywhere in Whitney. As they passed the Starbucks where Rosa always stopped for a treat after an appointment with her doctor, she swung on Lettie. "No way. Not Dr. Feldmann."

When Lettie didn't respond, Rosa said, "I'll take that as a yes. What the hell are you thinking? Is this some kind of an intervention? And just so you know, I'm not going in there."

Lettie was more calm than argumentative. "Yeah, you are Rosa. And yeah, I guess you could say it's an intervention of sorts. We're all deeply worried about you."

"Bullshit. What do you expect Feldmann to do—wave a magic wand and Ricky will appear?" Lettie pulled her red truck in the medical center's parking lot and put the vehicle in park, still not speaking. "You actually went behind my back and made an appointment with Feldmann." Incredulous, Rosa was shaking her head, unable to compute the deceit from her friend. "You've gone too far this time, Lettie. Way too far."

"Just so you know *I* didn't make the appointment, Rosa. Your husband did. But I volunteered to listen to your crap and drag your sorry ass over here."

"Terry? Terry made the appointment?" Rosa felt betrayed…and very, very pissed as tears sprung so fast she didn't have a chance to halt their flow. She spit out the distasteful words, "That son of a bitch."

Lettie yanked the keys from the ignition and unleashed a pent-up tirade on her longtime friend. "YOU are one lucky woman to have so many people worried and caring about you, especially a husband who loves you enough to risk your crazy-ass wrath. If you don't care about any of us, and you can't do this for yourself—walk through those doors and get healthy for Ricky. And by the way, you also have another son who is floundering in the fallout from this mess. So as you are always so quick to tell the rest of us, 'It's time to put on your big girl panties and get your life back in order.' " Lettie exited the truck, slammed the driver's door closed, and walked around the back of the vehicle to the passenger side. When she reached Rosa, she touched her shoulder through the open window. Her anger had subsided and she said, in a much more sympathetic tone, "Come on, honey. Let's go inside."

Looking at her friend, Rosa swiped tears with the palm of her hand as she sobbed, "I can't do this anymore, Lettie. It hurts so much. I just want to get rid of the pain."

"You only have to hang on a little bit longer, honey. We're going to help you get through this."

Chapter 5
Phree

The old convent had a closed-up odor—slightly musty, but mostly a dry and aged, lack-of-circulating-air smell. Maneuvering between the rooms in the maze that would someday be a quilters retreat, *her* quilters retreat, Phree opened windows. She invited the late spring freshness to spill into the building and force away years of staleness. The breeze that wafted in from open doors and windows prompted years of settled dust motes to gracefully pirouette through the rooms. "It'll be a new beginning for both of us, Old Girl," she said out loud to the building.

Phree strolled between the many rooms crafting page after page of to-do lists on a yellow legal pad, and leaving corresponding sticky notes on walls, windows, and floors. Rooms needed painting and patching, hardwood floors should be refinished and brought to a beautiful 'bowling alley' shine, several windows required replacing, and then so many things needed updating, especially in the out-of-date kitchen.

Teams of workers would begin the transition from convent to quilt retreat tomorrow, and she wanted to be prepared to discuss plans and ideas with the various tradesmen. Not only did the main building need a complete overhaul, so did the caretaker's house at the back of the property that Phree would soon call home. In addition, there was also a large maintenance building, several other storage type structures, a spacious chapel complete with stained glass windows, and what once had been a beautiful native fern grotto with a currently nonfunctioning man-made waterfall.

Flipping back to the first page, Phree printed in bold letters at the top of the page, "I want this to be a creative place and a peaceful haven that women will want to visit over and over." *Is that enough for a mission statement?* She hugged the yellow tablet to her chest as the soft scent of spring warmth blew over hundreds of miles of farmland from the south. Smiling she said, "My mission statement can be anything I want it to be. After all, *I'm* in charge here."

The list of garden ideas and questions for the landscaper seemed to grow with each step Phree took while walking the perimeter of the building. Determined daffodils randomly poked through massive tangles of weeds where spectacular flower beds must once have thrived. Stone paths were sorrowfully overgrown with grass, and a limitless amount of dandelions had completely devoured any sign of lawn on the west side of the building. Phree made a note that a crumbling concrete patio outside the sunroom could transition into a lovely bird feeding station; it would be perfect on snowy winter days. She could picture quilters sipping hot cocoa, coffee, or tea while watching the wild birds feast and skitter between a multitude of feeders.

The sound of rocks dinging off the underside of a vehicle brought her attention back to the moment. Assuming it was Bill, or Officer Hottie as the Bunco girls called him, she was both stunned and saddened by what she saw. The old-model, bright-yellow Beetle could only belong to one person, and right now that was the one person she *didn't* want to see.

Phree instinctively slipped her cell phone from her back pocket and looked at the time. It was 2:30 in the afternoon, too early for Bill, yet making dear old Mom, who preferred to be called Sunnie, two and a half hours late. It would take more than a few deep breaths for Phree to dislodge the disappointment from her heart that Sunnie had once again put her own needs before those of her daughter.

Phree couldn't stop herself, or the venom dripping from her serpent's tongue, when Sunnie open the car door. "Well, look who decided to show up. Too bad you're almost three hours late."

Expecting Sunnie's usual greeting when confronted about such things, a flap of her hand in front of her face along with a pfffff sound, and one of her usual excuses like, "You won't believe how busy I've been" or "the traffic was bad" or "if you didn't live so far away." Phree was surprised when, instead, Sunnie said, "I'm sorry, honey. I never seem to have time for you after I've been so wrapped up in helping everyone else. I'm afraid I haven't been a very supportive mother."

Huh, where did that *come from? Is she playing me?* Phree blinked several times but sure enough it was her mother, thin as always, numerous piercings covering her ears, and a tiny studded diamond in her nose. She was decked out in one of her signature deconstructed-recycled sweaters and frayed blue jeans with a big raggedy hole in one knee. Not having a clue what to say or how to react, Phree didn't respond at all to Sunnie's comment. Instead she simply said, "Come on. I'll show you around."

Phree's parents had been hippies. For the first eighteen years of her life, "home" had been an expansive yet somewhat run-down, U-shaped series of three-flats on Chicago's South Side. The families that worked at the complex occupied one section of the buildings and did so with an open-door policy. Each entry door to the six apartments had been removed from its hinges and stored in the musty basement. Replacing the traditional wooden doors were curtains of tie-dyed fabric, layers of beads, faded old quilts, or any combination of the three.

Sunshine, Wolf, and little Phreedom Aquarius Eaton lived in the egalitarian community complex known as City Care Chicago or CCC. The members of CCC did not live in the old '60s communal sense of free love and drugs. It was more of a co-op than a commune. Although as Phree grew older and became more aware of her surroundings, she noticed that Mr. Caraway was rather touchy-feely around Mrs. Evans. When they were together, they were both always very happy, which caused Mr. Evans to become extremely cranky. There were several occasions when she heard her father warning members, "This is unacceptable. It's not what we're about here. We can't help people with drug problems if our own members are using." Wolf had a rich, booming voice that complemented his name, and even when he was trying to be guarded, Phree often overheard him "howling" at members of his pack.

For the most part City Care Chicago was a community of like-minded people who wanted to help others, keep themselves away from big corporations, and live as simply as possible without interference. The families banded together to help the needy, the homeless, the abused, and an occasional runaway or mistreated child. On one hand Phree had enjoyed the spirit of CCC with its small community of families, but for the most part, while growing up, she felt isolated, alone, and sheltered from kids her own age.

Just days after Phree was presented with her homeschooled high school diploma, a drugged-out, smelly man held a knife to her throat when he disagreed with something her father had said. The incident lasted only a few minutes, but young Phree was left frightened and angry. A week later she moved in with her well-grounded grandmother, and registered for classes at the local community college. Phree loved the suburbs, loved going to college with all of the "normal" kids, and because she had grown up insulated and starved for socialization, she fell deeply in love with the first boy who asked her on a date.

What followed was a quick marriage, a wonderful baby girl, and a divorce that should have happened sooner than it did. Left penniless from her cheating, gambling ex-husband,

Phree eked out a living for herself and her daughter by selling items on eBay.

...And then one day the Mayflower discovery happened.

Hours passed as Phree gave her mother a detailed tour of the buildings. Bill had stopped by for a tour after his shift on the Whitney Police Department was finished for the day. He kept the stay short because he didn't want to intrude on Sunnie's visit. He had been well-mannered, and the couple had struggled to keep their hands off each other in front of her mother. But a little touch here, a light hand on the back there, and a short kiss on the cheek to say goodbye was all the information that Sunnie needed to put two and two together. Bill wasn't even to the parking lot when Sunnie said to her daughter, "Well, he's sure an improvement over Gary."

Phree felt like she was sixteen years old again, and her mom had just discovered her making out with the teenage boy who lived across the hall. She tried to play innocent. "What do you mean? We're just friends."

"Give me a break I'm not blind, Phree. The two of you emitted enough heat to start this place on fire."

Phree scoffed as she raised one shoulder up and let it drop. "So? It's no big deal...but I guess I kind of like him."

Putting an arm around her daughter's waist, Sunnie headed them both toward the next room. "We'll be talking about this later. I'd like to know more about Bill Hayden, and what's going on with you two."

While sharing ideas for the Mayflower Quilters Retreat, or the MQR as they were calling it for short, Phree was reminded of the only time she could remember spending quality time with her mother as an adult. It was when Sunnie fell to pieces after Wolf died. Mother and daughter had spent almost two weeks together while Sunnie attempted to face the transition of life without her beloved Wolf. Phree was in the middle of an ugly divorce from The Bastard, as the Bunco girls call her ex, and she had pleaded with Sunnie to spend some time with her and Emily. "Just a few weeks or maybe even a month or two. You can get to know your granddaughter, and we could support each other during these hard times." Phree hoped they could finally build a meaningful mother-daughter connection. But it was not to be. Sunnie immersed herself helping the needy in Wolf's memory at CCC, while her daughter suffered the multiple losses of both husband and father, not to mention her dreams. A bitter pill? *You bet your ass.* And Phree hardened once again toward the mother she had, while wishing for the one she needed.

But she had to give it to Sunnie, she was one hell of a creative person as ideas and thoughts flowed from her during the tour of the MQR. They ended the walk-through with a brainstorming session at one of the four large dining tables. Lined yellow pages from the legal tablets were spread out in front of them like a banquet of ideas, with sketches of rooms and lists of thoughts and concepts.

Phree glanced at her phone and was shocked at the time. "How about I order some dinner?" Assuming Sunnie would decline as usual, she wanted to beat her mother to the punch and imply that it didn't matter one way or the other if she accepted the dinner offer or not. "Unless, of course, you need to get home."

"No. And yes, I'd love to stay. Didn't you tell me you had a really good rib place down here a while back? It's been forever since I've had decent ribs."

Ms. Almost-vegetarian-verging-on-vegan was asking to stay for a rib dinner? "Are you serious?"

"Of course I am." Sunnie started to organize scraps and sheets of yellow lined paper into piles as she further shocked Phree by saying, "Why don't we take all this paperwork to your house? We can relax after dinner and go over a few more ideas that I have."

"Um, okay, but are you sure?"

Sunnie paused from her paper shuffling, raised her eyebrows, and gave Phree that mom look, the one conveying impatience. Punctuating each word, she said, "Yes, I'm sure. Call the rib joint and order us some dinner." Tapping the papers on the table to straighten the stack, she added, "Besides, I'm looking forward to seeing my granddaughter again."

"I admit I'm a little surprised that you actually ate ribs for dinner." Phree was licking the tangy orange sauce off her fingers and gave the pinky a detailed once-over. "Boy, that was good. Maybe we should order these for a special rib night at the MQR once in a while."

"That sounds like a fun idea. Maybe we should."

Phree noticed that Sunnie had said "we"—as though she would be part of a team to plan and order food for the retreat.

Sunnie pushed her chair back from the table. "Oh my goodness, I'm stuffed." She smiled, pursed her lips, and blew a slow stream of air from her mouth while patting her tummy. "Maybe while our dinner settles we could drive to the Dairy Queen for some ice cream. I think I'd like to try one of those Blizzards I hear people talking about. What do you think, Emily?"

Without thinking, Phree blurted, "Don't you need to be getting home soon?"

"Mooom," Emily said in a drawn-out, singsong voice. "Don't be so mean to Grandma. I never get to see her."

"All I meant," Phree sputtered defensively, "is that I know Sunnie doesn't like to drive in the dark."

"It's already way too late for me to drive home. I thought I'd just spend the night here. I figured I could lend a hand tomorrow morning when the workers show up at the retreat." She held her hands out, palms up. "You might need someone to help."

Phree's eyes darted around the room like those of a captured animal looking for a way to escape.

"Don't look so afraid," Sunnie said. "We'd make a good team."

"Please stay, Grandma," Emily begged. "Maybe you could spend a couple of days and go to the Honors Banquet with us next week. That'd be so cool. Dad never shows up to any of my school stuff anymore. He says he doesn't like being around Mom."

Resting her head on the tips of her splayed fingers, Phree massaged her forehead for a few seconds. Ignoring her daughter's last comment, she said, "What's going on here, Sunnie? What do you want?"

"Come on, Mom, Grandma just wants to…"

Phree removed her hands from shielding her face and thumped them on the tabletop with a little more force than she intended. "Emily, this is between your grandmother and me."

"And I don't get a say in any of this?" Emily argued back. "I never get to see Grandma. I thought it would be nice if she could stay for a while."

While Phree wanted to say, "Nice for who?" she kept the bitter comment to herself.

Instead, Sunnie, always the peacemaker, turned to Emily and said, "Your mom's had a long day, honey. Why don't you and I go get that ice cream? When we come back your mom and I can tell you all about our plans for the quilters retreat."

Phree literally squeezed her lips together to hold back her comments. *Our plans? Since when did my lifelong dream include Sunnie Eaton?*

She could not begin to consider what her mother was up to, and to be perfectly honest, wasn't sure she wanted to find out. As Phree scraped rib bones and a couple of teaspoons of uneaten coleslaw off the plates and into the garbage, a thought came to her. *Could Sunnie need money now that Wolf was gone?*

She had offered her mother half of the money from the Mayflower discovery, but Sunnie had refused. "Wolf left me enough to be comfortable, and anyway you know we never cared about possessions and money. I've got my community of friends who will help if I need anything." *Yeah, right,* she had wanted to say. Maybe Sunnie had found out just how willing the community was to help an old lady with no money. Phree chided herself. That really wasn't fair of her to say, since CCC's whole mission in life was to help the needy.

Money. That had to be what was going on. She'd give her mom a chunk of money, and Sunnie could go back to Chicago and pay it back to the community. *Whatever makes you happy, Sunnie.*

Chapter 6
Sunnie

Scraping the bottom of the waxed Blizzard cup with the long-handled red plastic spoon Sunnie said, "Wow that was good. I need to eat these more often. You say the Snickers one is your favorite, Em?" Spooning the last of the sweet treat into her mouth, she said, "Tomorrow night I'm going to try the Snicker's Blizzard, and I think I'll get a medium instead of a small. Let's all do that."

"Yeah, let's do that." Phree said with a hint of snarkiness. "Let's try that next time."

Sarcasm had seeped into Phree's remarks several times this evening, and Sunnie was unsure how to proceed with her plan. She needed her daughter to view her as an asset, and so far Phree clearly thought of her as a liability.

Emily picked up her backpack and slung it over her shoulder. "I've got a quiz tomorrow that I need to study for. I'm gonna head upstairs." She bent over Sunnie and kissed her cheek. "Goodnight, Grandma. I'm glad you're staying tonight. I'll see you tomorrow."

"Looking forward to it, hon."

Emily walked behind Phree who was sitting at the table and trailed her hand across her mother's back. "'Night Mom, I'm glad you got the convent. It's really exciting. I love you."

"Love you too, Em. See you in the morning."

Neither woman spoke until the sound of Emily's door shutting drifted downstairs. A beat later the thumping of quiet music signaled that they could talk in private.

"Let's relax in the family room while we go over some ideas." Sunnie picked up the stack of notes they had compiled at the convent earlier in the day. "How about a cup of tea or a glass of wine, dear?"

"I have a feeling it's going to be a wine kind of night." Phree gathered a corkscrew with a bottle of wine and then removed two wineglasses from the china cabinet. Tipping the bottle above each wineglass, she decanted just the right amount. Without speaking, mother and daughter raised their glasses and then clinked them together.

"Peace," Sunnie said and took a small sip. She didn't want the wine to get the better of her if she was going to go head-to-head with her daughter tonight. "It's been a big day for you. Would you prefer to relax instead of discussing the retreat tonight?"

Phree took a much longer sip of wine than her mother had, and immediately went back for another. Sunnie waited patiently for Phree to express herself. She could learn a lot about her daughter's thoughts by letting her speak first. Working with the needy for the past many decades and acting as a liaison between them and various agencies had given Sunnie a leg up on communicating with people.

Phree set her wineglass on the coffee table and placed her hands in her lap. Keeping the edge out of her voice and attempting to replace it with compassion, she said, "What's going on? All day you've been a different person."

Sunnie swirled the pale liquid in her glass and gazed at it long enough for Phree to add, "If you need money, you know that I'm happy to share with you."

Sunnie looked up and read confusion on her daughter's face. "Oh, Phreedom, it's not about money. It's never been about money for your father and me. I could live comfortably at CCC for the rest of my life. It's just that..." Sunnie didn't know how to proceed. It became alarmingly clear that it was easier helping someone else with their problems than knowing what to do about your own. "I...I had this idea, but now I can see it was foolish." Taking a big gulp of wine and looking directly into her daughter's eyes for a flicker of hope she said, "I'll spend the night and be out of your hair tomorrow."

Phree didn't comment, and it saddened Sunnie when she saw relief take the place of confusion in her daughter's tired eyes.

Chapter 7
Phree

Whirling to a sitting position, Phree said, "What in the world?" She brushed hair out of her eyes and squinted to check the clock. It was 6:30 a.m. and she still had a full half hour to sleep. Smelling coffee, hearing voices and then laughter, she understood that Emily and Sunnie were most likely bonding and very probably strategizing to extend Sunnie's stay.

As she scolded herself to be kinder to her mother, the hot water from the shower spilled over her body and felt downright therapeutic. Today was going to be an exciting new beginning, and it was coming at the perfect time. Emily was off to college in August, and Phree was hopeful that if all went smoothly she could have the MQR open and running sometime in late September or early October. Unfortunately, annoyance was creeping into her spirit that on such a big day, her mother was downstairs cozying up to Emily. *I need to focus. I've waited a long time for this day, and I don't want anything or anyone to spoil it. Draw Sunnie in. Make her think you want her to stay – that you* need *her to stay. As always, that will surely scare her away.*

"You two are up early," Phree said as she walked through the kitchen with a basket of dirty clothes heading for the laundry room.

"Grandma fixed me breakfast." Emily slid off the stool at the counter and hugged Sunnie. "I'm gonna head for the shower. Thanks, Gram. Breakfast was amazing."

Phree rolled her eyes. When was the last time Emily not only thanked her for breakfast, but paid her high praise for *any* meal? A splash of detergent, a twist of the dial, and Phree was stopped short. Clean, dry clothes that had been lined up in baskets for folding, had all been neatly folded and were waiting to be put away. *Sunnie.*

"You must have been up for hours making that amazing breakfast and folding all of our laundry." Phree knew that sounded a little unkind and a lot petty. She wished she had phrased it nicer, so she added, "Thanks."

"I wanted to spend a little time with Emily this morning before I had to leave."

"You make it sound like I'm kicking you out. You're welcome to stay. As a matter of fact I'd love to have you stay and help at the retreat today. Then we can order something for dinner and have those fancy Blizzards for dessert again." *That's way more cozy time than she bargained for. It ought to push her right out the door.*

Emily entered the kitchen with purse, backpack, and jangling car keys, "Can you believe there's only nine days left of school, and I'll finally be out of there? I thought I'd swing by the retreat after school in case you need help with anything. I can't wait to see all the stuff you're doing there. Will you be there, Grandma?"

"I'm planning on it, honey."

"And tonight—are you staying again?"

"It sounds like I am." Sunnie glanced toward Phree.

"Cool. I'll see you guys later." Emily hugged both women and was gone before Phree had time to realize what had just happened. She had sorely underestimated the connection that her daughter had with Sunnie.

Hugging her coffee cup with both hands, Phree sat across the table from her mother and said, "I'm glad you're staying." Phree thought it might be time to make peace with the disappointment she usually felt around her mom. Sunnie had not exactly been the mother Phree had needed, but they could enjoy each other as adults, couldn't they? It was time to show some kindness and forgiving. As always, she would be diligently cautious, as she waited for the other shoe to drop and for Sunnie to run off to a person who was at risk. But, yes, it was time, and she would hold out the olive branch toward Sunnie. "If you'd like to stay longer, we'd both love to have you."

Phree saw relief in Sunnie's eyes, as her face relaxed. "I'd like that very much. I want to be a part of your lives." Sunnie brushed leftover crumbs from breakfast into a little pile in front of her. "You've done a wonderful job with Emily. She's a great kid. You must be very proud of her."

Phree was slightly taken aback, but at the same time pleased. *Who didn't like a compliment from a parent, no matter what your age?* "Thanks, I am. That's nice of you to say."

"I'm also very proud of *you*, Phreedom. You've overcome a lot of crap in your life and still managed to stay focused on what's important."

If Sunnie was angling for a compliment as a mother, Phree *would* not, *could* not offer her one. Standing, she picked up her coffee mug and carried it to the sink. Keeping her back to Sunnie she wouldn't see sadness on her mother's face. She had, however, allowed a sliver of hope to seep into her heart that today could be the start of the mother-daughter bond she'd always wanted. While rinsing the breakfast dishes and loading the dishwasher, she said, "We should probably get going. The contractor will be at the retreat in about a half an hour."

"I'm so glad you invited me to stay, I'm really looking forward to helping any way I can for as long as you need me."

Sunnie's cell phone bleated out the tune to "The Age of Aquarius". Phree stood stock still when she heard Sunnie say, "Try to keep them both there. I'll be back in about an hour."

Phree's heart hardened. The warmth that had only moments ago run through her veins froze, as once again her mother had chosen someone over her.

Chapter 8
Rosa

"Thank God for antidepressants," Rosa said as she answered the door to Lettie's knock. "I really can't tell you how grateful I am that you were a huge pain in my ass that day."

"You're welcome…I think. How are you feeling?"

"It's been about two months since I started taking the magical happy pills. I'm still overwhelmed with sadness every day, but I feel like I'm able to cope a little better. I guess I'm hopeful again, and that's a big deal for me." Rosa closed the door behind Lettie. "Counseling has also helped both Terry and me a lot. I can't believe I thought I could handle this nightmare on my own."

"All of us are happy to see you back among the living. I know you're still suffering inside, but you've made huge progress in a short time. Beth told me she saw you at The Depot the other night when she stopped to pick up pizza for her family."

"It helps to remember that this has been tough on Terry, too. Sometimes as hard as it is to go to The Pizza Depot to work or check how Terry's holding up, I remind myself I'm getting healthy for the whole family. I'm also working on patching things up between Alex and me. I was so focused on Ricky and myself that I almost lost my other son, too. We're going to a White Sox game next week—just the two of us. We're having a Mommy-Alex day. That's what we used to call it when he was little and needed some Mom time. It's way too easy to overlook Alex because he's adult age and in college, but I lifted my head above the daze long enough to finally see that I was driving him away."

Lettie placed a hand on her friend's arm. "No matter how old he is, he'll always need his mom."

"How come you're so smart about kids? I've got two, but I still managed to overlook that important fact."

"I may not have children of my own, but once upon a time I was a kid myself, and I'm still able to remember what it was like at times." Helping herself to some M&M's from a candy dish, she said, "So what's the deal with these patterns you want me to look at? Tell me what's up before we get to the quilt shop."

Rosa led her friend to the kitchen table. Several patterns rested side by side, along with a small stack of quilt magazines that had several yellow sticky notes marking pages. "Marge suggested that I make a quilt for Ricky—a kind of birthday present / peace offering quilt. Two weeks from today will be his fifteenth birthday. I thought if I occupied myself by making a gift for him and then kept visualizing when I'd give it to him, it might help me get through his birthday without him."

"That's actually a pretty good idea," Lettie said. "Marge is, and always will be, an enigma to me. While half the time she drives us crazy, the other half we don't know what we'd do without her."

"I went through my stash and pulled out a few patterns that I thought might work, but I'm also open to looking for a new pattern at the Quilter's Closet. It's got to be masculine," Rosa said. "One thing for sure, with all he's been through, Ricky is not a little boy anymore." The two friends discussed the possibilities of the patterns, while mulling over potential color palettes and fabric styles. "Helen's working at the quilt shop today. That's why I want go there this afternoon."

Being with Lettie, seeing Helen, and getting out of the house and away from her thoughts left Rosa feeling somewhat rejuvenated. Helen's enthusiasm for quilting was contagious, and Rosa walked out of the Quilter's Closet with two large bags of patterns and fabric. It was Helen's turn to host Bunco next month, and Rosa made a personal deadline to have the top of Ricky's quilt pieced together by then for show-and-tell. A deadline would keep her working and help to keep her honest.

Several piles of yummy fabric, a stack of coordinated fat quarters, three new patterns, spools of various colors of thread, and a package of new rotary blades rested on Rosa's sewing table. Fanning out the cuts of cloth she regrouped them by quilt design into three new piles and placed the corresponding pattern on top of each stack. Spools of colored thread topped off each collection, as though they were crowned with jewels.

With Lettie gone and the frenzy of fabric shopping over, Rosa sat alone with her elbow on the table and chin in hand. She felt overwhelmed by the projects in front of her. These same projects, only seven months ago, would have made her giddy with anticipation, but now prompted indifference. She pulled all three patterns out of their stacks and gazed at the photos of the finished pieces. Which one would Ricky like? Randomly choosing one of the quilt designs, with a Herculean effort, she reluctantly unzipped the plastic bag that held the pattern. What had seemed like such a good idea only hours ago was turning into a project too big for her to bear. She thought of her self-imposed deadline, and then pictured Ricky back home lying under her creation.

As Rosa calmed her breathing she repeated over and over in her head, "Do this for your son. Find yourself for the sake of the family. One baby step at a time."

Chapter 9
Sunnie

Crap, crap, crap. Her daughter was angry with her—again. But what seemed even worse to Sunnie was the depth of her daughter's disappointment. Sunnie had tried to explain to Phree that this would be the perfect opportunity to gather some of her clothes and a few items she might need for a longer stay. But Phree threw her hands up with disgust and said, "Go. Just go. I can take care of my life just fine without you. I'm used to it by now."

Pulling the old Beetle into its parking space in the alley behind CCC, Sunnie's heart felt heavy in her chest, chained to a ton of mother-guilt that she couldn't overcome. She'd sort out what was going on with these street kids and put someone else in charge of the case. More than ready to hand the baton to another community member for good, she'd call an emergency meeting of City Care Chicago and tender her resignation. She would explain that she wanted to spend time with her daughter and granddaughter. But at this moment, Sunnie needed to focus on the emergency that waited for her inside.

As she closed the door to her car, she forced herself to remember what Dan had told her when he called. There were two boys, both claiming to be eighteen years old; one of the boys brought a very ill friend in for help. Most likely the boy was sick from either eating spoiled food from the garbage or possibly appendicitis. Dan suspected one of the boys was probably not yet eighteen.

Entering the infirmary at City Care Chicago, Sunnie was met with the familiar odor of unwashed clothes and bodies and then the overwhelming stench of illness. Sliding an exam glove onto each hand, Sunnie said to Dan as they walked down a hall toward the sickbed, "Bring me up to speed."

"Shark is running a fever of 102.3. Vomiting, diarrhea, cramps." Dan looked relieved that she had arrived and let out a pent-up breath. "He refuses to see a doctor or go to the clinic or hospital." They continued at a fast pace to a room that held several cots with clean white sheets. The boy lay on one of the cots, shivering and covered with blankets. "I don't think this has to do with drugs or an overdose. The kid that brought him in was real scared. He took off, but said he'd check in later to see how Shark was doing."

Bending over the boy as she brushed a greasy clump of hair from the youngster's cheek, she said in a calm and soothing voice, "Hi, Shark. My name is Sunnie, and I'm here to help you, honey."

"Keep him quiet. We need to get as many liquids in him as possible," Sunnie told Dan, as she snapped off the blue exam gloves. "Dr. Scott agrees that it's probably from bad food. Shark admits to eating some awful smelling food about twelve hours ago behind the diner down the street." Dr. Scott was one of the volunteer docs who took phone calls from CCC with simple medical emergencies and questions.

"So the usual," Dan said, "Ice chips, water, graduating to 7-UP, and then clear broth. How long should we keep him here if he agrees to stay?"

"This kid was pretty bad. He won't be going anywhere for a while." Sunnie sat at a desk in the infirmary and rummaged through forms until she found the one she was looking for. "Let's try to keep him for a few days, if we can. I'd like to get some healthy food in him and build up his strength a little before he heads back to the streets. At the very least, I want to make sure his urine is clear before he leaves."

"The kid who brought him in is waiting out front. Do you want to talk to him, or if you need to get back to your daughter's, I can take over?"

Sunnie thought of Phree for the first time since she drove the Beetle into its parking spot over two hours ago. "No, I'd like to talk to him and see what he has to say. This is the one that you think is probably underage?"

"Yeah. I'd be shocked if he's even sixteen." Runaways learned very quickly that the legal age to leave home was eighteen—anything younger than that, and by law, the police had to be called. Therefore, most of the runaways who showed up at CCC claimed to be at least eighteen.

Sunnie and Wolf had desperately tried to help anyone in need. They had hoped to change their little corner of the world for all the disadvantaged people. Sadly, there were just as many, if not more, runaways, abused women and children, and homeless people as when Wolf and she had started City Care Chicago all those years ago. With a tired sigh, Sunnie stood to greet yet another lonely, lost, and scared kid.

The boy sat in a chair with his elbows on his knees and his head hanging low, jiggling his feet up and down as if he had a nervous twitch.

"Hi there, I'm Sunnie."

When she spoke, he sprung to a standing position. His eyes dashed around the room looking for, but not finding, a threat of any kind. She knew better than to ask his name at this point, and holy cow, Dan was right, this guy had to be only fourteen or maybe fifteen years old at the most.

"Your friend is going to be fine. He's just had a bout with some bad food and is very dehydrated. We're going to let him rest and eventually get some healthy food into him."

"Did you call the cops?"

"We only do that if someone is dangerous, on drugs, or underage. From what I understand you both claim to be eighteen." Sunnie sat across from the boy, and he reluctantly sat down. "How about we get you something to eat, and you can tell me what happened to your friend. He's pretty sick and couldn't communicate very well." *Not entirely true, but I'd like to get this kid talking.* "Come on, let's go to the kitchen and see what we can find. I'm hungry, too."

The boy hesitated. He looked toward the exit door and then back at Sunnie.

"I didn't call the police, and I'm not going to." Sunnie put her hands on her hips like any impatient mom would do, conveying a motherly persona. "You said you're eighteen but have lost your ID, you're not on drugs, and you don't appear to be dangerous. Unless one of those three things changes, you've got nothing to worry about. Now let's go." She turned her back on him, expecting to be followed like a mother goose. There was a long hesitation, but Sunnie kept walking and eventually heard his footsteps as he trailed behind. "Why don't you tell me your name, so I have something to call you."

"Cardo. Everyone calls me Cardo."

Chapter 10
Phree

The sun was beginning to burn off a light fog that had settled deep into the woodland behind the Mayflower Quilters Retreat. Birds of every color skimmed between the trees calling to a mate or looking for something to eat. An army of robins, fresh from their northward migration, marched across the lawn, heads cocked toward the earth, listening for a meal. Phree closed the car door behind her as she filled her lungs with the early morning air—fresh and full with the scent of dew on grass.

The transformation begins today. I need to get my disappointment with Sunnie out of my head and focus on myself—my dream – my future.

She leaned her butt on the front of her van and folded her arms across her chest. Standing here, looking at the old convent, the caretaker's home, and this beautiful chunk of property *should* have made her heart pick up speed. But instead, her heart felt heavy. Heavy with the disappointment of yet one more time being brought up to the brink of hope only to be let down again. *When will I learn? Am I acting like a spoiled child instead of an adult? Why does it still hurt me so much?* If she had had plans with one of her friends and something came up that they needed to attend to—she would understand. It wouldn't be an issue. Why did she make such a big deal out of every perceived slight from Sunnie?

Tilting her head back to stare into the pure cerulean sky, she took a deep cleansing breath, and thought, "You've got two options, girly. Either keep trying to woo Sunnie, or write her off."

The sound of a vehicle driving down the lane to the parking lot pulled Phree back to the moment. Pushing herself upright off the front of her new van, she said out loud, "Focus. Compartmentalize. Think about Sunnie another time."

After exiting his pickup, the contractor offered his hand to Phree. "I'm Josh Williams. Nice to meet you, Ms. Clarke." He was clad in the mandatory plaid flannel shirt with clean, but work-worn blue jeans.

"Please, call me Phree. We're going to be seeing a lot of each other. No need to be so formal."

"My father and partner, Nate, is finishing a job in Park Forest. He'll be joining the team in two or three days." Josh swept his arm toward the convent, shirtsleeves rolled to the elbow. "Shall we get started? I can't wait to hear what we'll be doing in there."

As they walked toward the building, Phree brought him up to speed with her intentions for the compound.

"I have to admit, I've never worked on a project for a quilters retreat before. But I'm confident that we can successfully turn this group of buildings into your vision." Josh had coffee-with-cream colored skin, gray eyes, dreads pulled back into a fat ponytail, and a great bod. Sexy.

"Your company came highly recommended by Bud Russell, the husband of a good friend of mine. Bud told me not to work with anyone else on this type of job."

"I appreciate that. Bud's about the best electrician you'll ever find, and I'm glad he'll be on board with us."

As they entered the domed marble foyer, Josh let out a long low whistle. "Holy moly, this is going to be fun."

Even though Josh claimed to know nothing about quilting, he was soon offering suggestions that Phree hadn't yet considered, as he coaxed information about her expectations of day-to-day life at the retreat. "Where do you envision your general manager's office going?"

"Well, I'm not sure." The truth was she had never given a thought to hiring a GM. She assumed she'd just run the whole place herself. Not wanting to appear as though she had no idea what she was doing, she said, "I guess it could go in any of these spaces. What do you think would work best?"

He pointed to the biggest of several office spaces that was closest to the front door, "I'd put her in this space." Snapping a shiny tape measure from his belt, Josh wrote the dimensions on the rough drawing he had made of the bottom floor of the building. "We could line this area with five-foot filing cabinets, and then put a built-in credenza over here with shelving or cabinets above." He stepped toward the window in the room. "This would be the perfect spot for the GM's desk. Do you think you'll need additional file and storage space?" He didn't wait for an answer. "I assume you'll have surveillance on the outside doors of the retreat and the entrance to the driveway. Will the feed come into this office?" When Phree didn't answer, Josh stopped his note-taking and looked up at her.

"I'm...I'm afraid I don't know what in the hell I'm doing." She took her cheater glasses from her nose and let them dangle on the artsy chain that held them around her neck. "I know what I want...or at least I *thought* I knew what I wanted as far as the needs of quilters and a world class retreat for them, but I never gave much thought to the running of this place." Phree felt really, really naïve. "Kind of dumb, huh?"

"Nah, I can get a little carried away with the minutiae. I tend to have a vision of the function and potential of a space, and get ahead of myself." Clicking the tape measure back onto his belt he said, "There's plenty of time for details. Why don't we go room by room and discuss the purpose of that specific area, while I check for any structural problems. You tell me your ideas, and I'll bounce some thoughts off you. Eventually we'll get everything nailed down, but for today let's just think about the big picture." He led her back to the hallway, where he said, "Shall I mark this as the GM's office?"

"Perfect." Walking across the foyer to a near mirror image of the GM's office, she opened the heavy wooden door. "I was thinking this room would be a store or minimarket of sorts. I'd like to have a very small section for personal items like lip balm, deodorant, tissues, hand lotion, shampoo, toothpaste, and maybe even cough medicine and Tylenol—that kind of stuff, but very limited." She felt reassured when she saw that Josh approved by taking notes. "For the rest of the space I plan to have some quilting supplies for sale. Again, a minimal amount. I know the owner of the local quilt shop, and we've briefly discussed items such as sewing machine needles, threads, gadgets, rulers, some fat quarters, maybe a…"

The contractor interrupted her flow of words. "Did you say *fat* quarters? What's that?"

Phree laughed, "Yes—fat quarters. It's a quilting term for a measurement of fabric. They're not very big, but they can come in handy if a quilter needs a bit of fabric." At this point she thought it best not to mention jelly rolls, layer cakes, or other odd "food" names for fabric collections, which she also intended to stock in the little shop.

"May I ask your plans on who will run the shop?" Josh knit his eyebrows and then said, "Have you thought about owning the shop yourself as part of the retreat and keeping the profits instead of involving the local quilt shop?"

"I know this will be hard to believe, but I'm going to put something like a cigar box on the counter. Sales will be done on the honor system. For the most part, quilters are honest people, and I'm convinced it would be unheard of for any of my guests to steal from the retreat." Josh nodded, but Phree saw the 'you're-out-of-your-freaking-mind' look on his face. "As far as stocking the shop itself, I *couldn't* and *wouldn't* take business away from our local shop, the Quilter's Closet. Sandy has worked hard and sacrificed to build her business into a regional destination for quilters. Do you know that an average of two busloads of quilters pass through her shop each week? No, our agreement is fine. We have some details to work out, but I'm happy with our arrangement."

Josh nodded unconvincingly at the plan and walked over to one of the two windows. Pushing on the wooden window frame, attempting to open it, and then jotting on his tablet, he said, "This one needs replacing." He then pointed to the floor. "You can see where it has leaked over the years. We can fix the floor with re-sanding and a little polyurethane, and then replace the plaster wall where it got wet."

They continued the tour through the main floor, leaving the kitchen until last. Josh's list had grown to several pages and entering the kitchen he said to Phree, "I've got to be honest, I'm surprised this building is in such good shape. Between its age and after being vacant for so long, I expected to see much more damage. From what I can tell at this point, the building appears to be sound and fairly well insulated. I don't see any need to take down walls and reconfigure rooms, do you?"

"I figure the rooms will suit our needs just fine the way they are."

"Also, I definitely agree with your plan for installing new high-efficiency, water-saving toilets and modernizing the style of all thc sinks and vanities. With updated paint colors and more contemporary design elements, I'd say you will have an impressive retreat."

Phree allowed herself to smile and felt some tension leave her clenched jaws. "I'm afraid this kitchen is going to take the most work." She walked toward a small standard-size, four-burner stovetop. "While I have some vague ideas what might be needed in here, I don't have any knowledge of how to design an efficient kitchen that will be able to kick out three meals a day, plus snacks, for up to 50 people."

"My team and I work hand in hand with a woman, Claire Givens, who handles all aspects of interior design but specializes in kitchens and baths. Let's pull her onto the job and get her opinions." Again, the bright yellow tape measure was sent uncoiling and chiming across the old linoleum floor. The size of the room was recorded on the growing list of notes. Josh opened the door toward the back of the kitchen. "Whoa, this is one heck of a pantry—huge." He disappeared inside, and Phree once again heard the familiar sound of his tape measure being unleashed.

She was beginning to feel overwhelmed with the numerous tasks ahead of her. A panicky sweat covered Phree's body as her mouth went dry, and she swabbed her upper lip with the back of her hand. She rather liked the idea of someone helping with the interior design of the retreat and especially the kitchen.

Josh emerged from the pantry and said, "I think that about does it for the main level…unless you've got any questions or thoughts at this point."

Phree shook her head, "No, I'm good."

"Well, then, shall we head upstairs?" Josh did a double take. "You look a little pale. Are you all right?"

"Nothing more than a full-blown panic attack, but I'll be fine. I suspect it won't be the last one you witness from me while on this job site."

"Are you sure you don't want to sit down for a few minutes? I've seen this happen before with clients. It's really not that unusual."

"Really, I'm fine. Let's take a look at the sleeping quarters upstairs."

With more confidence than she felt, Phree led Josh up the dimly lit stairway in the back of the kitchen to the bedroom/sleeping area. On the way upstairs, she explained that she wanted an elevator to the second floor. "I thought these back stairs would be a good place for an elevator except for the fact that people would have to walk through the kitchen to get to it."

"You have a huge building here, and I'm pretty sure I can find a better place for your elevator. We can keep the back stairs for housekeeping and a fire exit only. That way, in an emergency anyone upstairs would have two ways to get downstairs and outside."

At that moment, Phree thought Josh was not only patient and gorgeous to look at, but brilliant to boot.

Chapter 11
Rosa

Rosa's husband made lazy figure eights on her back with the palm of his hand, and said, "Why don't you call Phree and tell her you're not having a good day and can't make it? I'm sure they'd all understand."

Swiping at her eyes, Rosa said, "I *know* they'd understand. But I *also* know I need to be there…I just…it's so…I don't want to…" More tears flowed as Rosa tried to explain that she just wanted to be left alone and not have to socialize. Yet she was also aware that it would be best if she could force herself to show up at Phree's meeting to get her mind off both of her sons by helping someone else.

"Ricky's gone, and Alex hates me."

"Alex doesn't hate you. But we can't forget that his life also changed when Ricky ran away."

"He told me today that 'I need to get over it.' How can he be so glib? Does he think I can put Ricky out of my mind, out of my life, and simply 'get over' him?"

"I suppose he misses his brother as much as we do, but he also misses our family the way it used to be. Alex is only here for the summer. He'll be back in college in a few short months by the middle of August. I think we both need to make him feel loved, and that he's as important to us as Ricky."

"But why does he…" Rosa wasn't sure where to go with her thoughts. "He's an adult, Terry. Can't he understand we're devastated? Just how we would feel if *he* were the one missing."

"He's still our child, and he needs us. I'm sure he's aware that we're completely devastated. As is he. But he needs our reassurances, Rosa. *We're* the adults. We need to be strong for both of our boys." Terry took both of her hands. "Baby steps, Rosa. Go help Phree and the rest of the Bunco girls figure out what is going to happen at that retreat of hers. You've always had good ideas for stuff like that. I'll bet you've got some thoughts already, don't you."

Nodding her head, Rosa sniffled and said, "I might have a few ideas."

"Come on then, let's go. Do you want me to drive you?"

"No, you need to get back to The Depot, and I need to quit being pathetic. I have to remember that I'm doing this for Ricky," she paused for a beat, "and Alex. I want to be able to help Ricky when he gets back home. And I really, really need to be a better mom for Alex." *But what if Ricky never comes home? What if I don't ever see him again and never know what happened to him?* There it was—the thought that ran through her head dozens of times a day and crippled her to the point of emotional paralysis.

"Once you get to the retreat, you'll get caught up with all the planning and ideas, and I'm sure you'll have a good time. Knowing that group of women, you won't come home hungry, either."

"I know you're right—I *know* it, but it's so hard to motivate myself to be around other people."

"None of this is easy, especially for a mother, but we have to stay the course while we wait for our son to come home. He *will* come home, Rosa. I know he will."

"You're so strong, and I'm such a mess. How can you be so patient with me?"

"You've always been the heart of this family. You're our anchor. The person we all come to for everything and anything. Maybe it's just time for you to lean on me for a change." Terry put his arm around his wife. She snugged into his embrace and felt sheltered from her wretched reality for a few short moments. "We *will* get our son back, and when we do I have no doubt that you will take the reins of this family and steer us in the right direction."

"I pray you're right, because I don't think I can live like this much longer."

The Bunco girls were all asked to arrive at the retreat around 5:30. Rosa left her house at 5:30 sharp with two large bags of cheesy breadsticks that Terry had delivered to her from The Pizza Depot. If she was about ten or fifteen minutes late, Marge would be champing at the bit to get the meeting started, and Rosa could avoid spending chit-chatty, one-on-one time with everyone. She actually *did* have some ideas she wanted to share with the group. As she pulled down the long drive of the old convent, she spied everyone's cars already in the parking lot. Sunnie's unmistakable Beetle was there, too. *So far, so good.*

Taking her time walking to the front door, she began to feel an escalating level of excitement. Phree's notion of turning this lonely and vacant building into a quilters retreat was a wonderful idea, and any other time in her life she'd be thrilled to be included in the planning stages. Her friend was deserving of a successful venture, and Rosa felt happy for her—truly happy. *I'm surprised to feel joyful about anything. Terry was right, this will be good for me.*

The other women were starting to seat themselves at one of the large wooden tables when Rosa entered the dining room. Most of her friends carried plates piled high with food from the buffet, and the inviting fragrance of scented candles filled the space. Marge approached her with several handouts and a manila folder with her name on it. "Glad you could make it, honey. How are you feeling?"

"About the same. I'm hanging in there."

Taking The Pizza Depot bags from Rosa, she said, "I'll take care of these, you get yourself something to eat. We're about to start the meeting. I saved you a seat next to me."

The room was humming with voices as the women chatted with those seated next to them. They all said a quick hello to Rosa, and some held out a hand to grasp as she walked past, a wordless offering of support and solidarity. As she sat next to Marge and scooted her chair under the table, Rosa felt Lettie's evaluating gaze watching her closely. Her best friend was looking for telltale signs of despair and depression. Rosa sent a reassuring but somewhat wobbly smile across the table for Lettie's sake, but was positive her longtime friend would notice that her eyes were redder than usual.

"Ladies," Phree said, "I want to thank each of you for coming here to help me with ideas for the Mayflower Quilters Retreat. You're the most creative group of people I know, and I'm looking forward to hearing your thoughts. I'll quickly bring you up to speed with what has taken place over the past few days after meeting with the contractors and workers involved in this project." Phree looked toward Marge. "As you all know, Bud Russell will be spearheading all things electrical at the MQR. Bud recommended the father and son team, the Williams Group, for the job of head contractor, and…" She leaned forward and placed her palms flat on the table and in a conspiratorial fashion said, "I haven't met the father yet, but let me tell you the son, Josh, is a sight to behold—as in gorgeous."

"Uh-oh, do I detect competition for Officer Bill?" Lettie said.

"Nah. Josh is *very* married and has three little kids. But he'll be a nice diversion during the time the retreat is torn up." At this point, Phree launched into the various strategies and timetables for the retreat. "We are focusing these first few days on the MQR. Nate, Josh's father, will be finishing up his current project by next week, and he will spearhead all the work that needs to be done on the caretaker's home out back. That building apparently didn't have much attention paid to it over the years and will require a complete overhaul."

Rosa found herself intrigued with the brief synopsis of the construction plans that Phree shared with the group.

At the end of the summary, Phree said, "The crew and I are confident that the MQR will be open for business by the first of October." She paused for a moment. "I'd like to toss out the first agenda up for discussion tonight. You've all told me in one way or another that you would like to be somewhat active here at the retreat. I've been toying with how we could do that, and one of the most important things I need is trusted input. Since I truly don't know what the heck I'm doing, I'd like to invite you all to be on the Board of Directors for the Mayflower Quilters Retreat. We'd meet once a month—possibly more during these initial summer months. We'll concentrate on solving any problems or concerns, but most importantly determine a direction for the retreat. I understand if any of you aren't interested. I promise there will be no hard feelings."

Rosa busied herself with a paper clip so she wouldn't have to make eye contact with anyone, and hoped she didn't look as horrified as she felt. *I don't want to make any promises…any…to anyone.* But when it was her turn to commit, she looked directly at Phree, smiled, and said, "Of course, I'd be happy to accept."

After the appointments and unanimous consent by everyone, Phree continued with the evening's agenda. "I've already discussed some specific details with a few of you." Rosa noticed that Beth and Helen were nodding their heads. "With cooperation from the Quilter's Closet, we are planning a small retail room which will be stocked with a limited amount of fabrics, mostly fat quarters and notions such as needles, thread, scissors and so forth." Phree swept her hand toward Helen. "Helen will keep the boutique stocked and be the liaison between the Quilter's Closet and the MQR. If an item is not on hand, quilters can place orders, and Helen will fill and deliver them as needed."

Rosa joined the rest of the women as they bobbed their heads and agreed that this was a great idea. Phree continued, "I want the quilters who are guests at the MQR to be able to further pamper themselves if they choose to do so. In the planning is a space for a mini-salon/spa. Beth has agreed to run the salon one day a week. She'll offer color, cuts, manicures, and pedicures. For one or two other days during the week, depending on demand, the space will be available for massages and facials. I need to find an amazing masseuse. If any of you know someone, I'd be grateful for their contact information."

Marge said, "Amy in Las Vegas was fabulous. Do you think we could talk her into moving to Illinois?"

The women laughed, and Phree said, "I think that's a little unlikely."

"Joking aside," Marge continued, "I've been getting a massage every two weeks since we got back from Vegas, and the woman I go to is very good. I'll e-mail her contact info to you."

"That would be great, Marge, thanks." Phree's cheeks puffed with air and she let a long breath escape. "So I'm wondering if any of you would be interested in joining the MQR in any capacity. I'm thinking primarily of instructors for classes or seminars, but any thoughts are welcome at this point. Also, there will be no hard feelings if you aren't interested in becoming involved, or if you should change your mind and need to leave for any reason. I know we're all busy with our own lives. Oh, that reminds me, I've decided to have a general manager to take care of the daily grind of running this place. So, if any of you know of a capable woman, preferably with quilting knowledge, please let me know. I'll share the big office by the front door with her. I've requested that Josh give that space top priority so we can get moved in and start with the planning and scheduling of the retreat."

Phree nodded and pointed with her hand, palm up, toward her mother. "You've all met my mom at one time or another. Sunnie will have an active role here at the MQR. We haven't nailed down exactly what she'll be doing yet, but with her creativity, there should be several different ways to plug in to her resourcefulness."

"I, for one, would love to know how to make those recycled sweaters and sweater coats that you create from unwanted sweaters. Maybe others would also enjoy a workshop or class teaching those techniques, too," Lettie said.

"That's one of the classes Sunnie and I have been discussing," Phree told the group. "I was thinking a week that featured 'wearables' would be the perfect slot for Sunnie's sweaters."

Nedra leaned forward, and with her elbow on the table waggled her manicured fingers to get Phree's attention. "Are you planning on a newsletter of some kind? Have you thought about a presence on the social media sites? We should have a Web site with class information and the pricing structure, and a blog would be fun, too. I'd love to volunteer to sink my teeth into the written and internet end of the retreat. That is, if you'd like me to."

Rosa thought this was a fabulous use of Nedra's talents. As the Assistant-to-the-Editor at *Excel Chicago Magazine*, she could write circles around anyone.

"Ned, I hadn't even given any thought to that aspect of marketing the retreat. But, yes, I love your ideas and I accept your offer. Not as a volunteer, though. You'll all get paid if you are working for the retreat."

Nedra made a pffft sound and fanned her hand in front of her face. "No need. It will be fun."

"That may be true, but I'm looking to build a lasting team for the retreat—not a bunch of freebies from my friends. Don't get me wrong, the pay probably won't be anywhere near what your skills are worth, but it will be a nice chunk of change to spend on fabric or whatever you like."

"And can't all of us use more fabric for our stashes?" said Nancy.

"I'm excited about maintaining the little quilt shop, but I'd also love to do an applique class if that works into the plans," Helen said.

"Of course it would, Helen. Thank you." Phree jotted a note on her ever-present tablet of lined yellow paper.

"I would be happy to be involved teaching weaving or spinning," Lettie said. "Heck, maybe there could be a week-long retreat just for spinners, weavers, loomers, and knitters. I could teach hand-dyeing techniques, felting, and other fiber art - related procedures. I know several talented fiber artists who would probably also love to be involved. We could even work in a field trip to my studio."

"Great idea! I love it," Phree said.

Rosa envied the pure delight she saw on Phree's face. She felt happy for her friend, and longed for the day when she could feel such joy again.

Getting caught up in the enthusiasm, Rosa surprised herself when she announced, "I don't know if all of you are aware that I stared work on a quilt for when Ricky comes home. Marge gave me the idea, and I've found it very therapeutic." Rosa looked at Marge and smiled. "I was thinking maybe we could do a week retreat or even a short seminar for various community service projects. There are a lot of us who love making quilts, but have gotten to the what-am-I-going-to-do-with-one-more-quilt phase. I wouldn't mind spearheading something like that."

"What a wonderful idea," Phree said, and Rosa noticed the women were smiling and agreeing.

Sunnie spoke for the first time. "We would always welcome quilts at City Care for the abused women and children we help. Think how it would make them feel to know someone cared enough to make them a quilt."

Beth said, "I know the retirement community where Dad lives has an active quilting circle, and I bet they'd love the opportunity to come over for a 'day camp' to help out sometime."

"There's Project Linus, where handmade quilts go to critically ill children, and also Quilts of Valor for combat service members and veterans who are touched by war," Marge said.

"I think the idea of giving back is powerful and wonderful. Since most quilters are already giving-types, I bet it would be a big hit." Phree scribbled more notes, and Rosa enjoyed feeling that she might have just found a niche where she could turn her sadness into something positive.

"I'd love to teach a class," Nancy said. "After all, I *am* a teacher, but I don't have a clue what kind of class I could offer."

At the same time, four women said, "Your friendship quilt!"

"Oh my God, I never thought of that." Nancy had designed a friendship quilt honoring her friends in the Bunco Club. She had surprised the group last March when it was finished. All the women wanted to make one, and while Rosa hadn't started hers yet, it was on her to-do pile. "Yes, that's it! I could teach a class about my own specialized friendship quilt."

"Speaking of friendship quilts reminds me of something," Phree said. "I was thinking of using the Friendship Star quilt block as our logo. I'm going to have a large block painted on the outside of the building—like the way Lettie has it done on her studio barn. It will be on the end of the retreat that faces the parking lot, so when quilters drive up it should be one of the first things they notice."

"That's a fabulous idea. We can also use it as a logo on all of our printed and internet material. I'll get some images ready, and we can discuss colors and size." Nedra made a note on her computer tablet while the other women voiced approval and excitement over the idea.

"We all love anything visual," Nancy said.

"I have an idea, but I'd like to speak with Phree alone," Marge said.

"No way." Lettie shook her head. "We've all talked about our plans and gave our opinions in front of everyone. You're just going to have to man up and tell your ideas to all of the newly appointed board members. No secrets here."

"Yeah." Rosa found her opinionated voice. "You know secrets are not going to fly with this group."

Marge sputtered, "It…That…That is, it might be awkward for Phree."

Phree said, "Go ahead. They'll all find out anyway. That's why we're having this open forum."

Rosa knew that Marge, the Sarge, liked to be in control at all times, yet she had clearly misjudged this situation. She was stuck in an uncomfortable position and would have to fess up in front of everyone whatever was on her mind.

"Well, if you all insist." Straightening her back and shoulders as though she were bracing for a verbal battle, Marge shocked the whole room into silence when she said, "I'd like to apply for the position of General Manager of the Mayflower Quilters Retreat."

Chapter 12
Phree

Phree hoped her face didn't betray the *oh-shit* thought that just went through her stunned brain. She probably should say something gracious like, "That would be wonderful, Marge" or an enthusiastic, "Yes, let's do it." Instead what came out of her mouth was, "But what about your job? You've already got a career, and the GM position is full-time."

Marge looked painfully embarrassed, as did all of the other women sitting around the table. In pure Marge style, she approached the embarrassing moment head-on and with full eye contact. "I know, Ladies of the Board, but I'm 57 years old. While I love my job at the hospital, I'm getting burned out being an oncology nurse. This would be a dream job for me. How many more times in my life will an opportunity like this come around? You know I'm the queen of organizing and I can easily facilitate any group or event that is put in front of me. I could do this—I'd *LOVE* to do this." Marge's shoulders fell just a bit and for a wink of a moment she looked down at the table. "I know you all call me The Sarge. So, what better type of person can you think of for the position of general manager than a Sarge type? And to sweeten the pot, I have a master's degree in nursing. Surely, I'd be a handy person to have around."

Phree was quickly running down her own mental laundry list of reasons why Marge should or should not be her new GM. On a positive note, she was friends with and already knew Marge Russell, and for the most part, liked her. She was trustworthy, dependable, honest, and to top it off Marge was an exceptional quilter. How long would she have to look to find someone with all those qualifications? Even though there were times when Marge drove her and all the other women crazy, wouldn't that be the case with someone else...and maybe even worse? As the saying went, 'The devil you know is better than the devil you don't know.' Phree said, "We haven't even discussed a salary yet."

"It's not about money," Marge said. "Having this job is about my psyche...my spirit."

"Good answer," Phree said. "You're hired. When can you start?"

Applause, whoops, and congratulations came from all the women sitting around the table as Phree and Marge walked toward each other, shook hands, and then sealed the deal with a hearty embrace.

Phree was flying high after the successful meeting with her friends. "You go ahead, Sunnie, Em's waiting at home for us. The two of you can bond while you set the table for dinner." Walking her mother toward the door, she said, "I'll be home shortly with the Chinese food."

Sunnie walked out of the retreat with the rest of the women, linking arms with Marge, and congratulating her on being the new general manager of the MQR.

Phree took a few moments to walk the length of the bottom floor. Happy, proud, and exhilarated, she was aware that the only other time she had felt this euphoric was when Emily had been born. Turning the key to lock the heavy wooden door behind her, she walked into rural darkness and clicked on her ever-present flashlight. She mentally added 'outdoor lighting' to the ASAP list. Flickering fireflies signaled the end of the day, while frogs and crickets croaked an evening melody. She couldn't wait until morning, when she could come back and work side by side with the tradesmen, as her dream slowly turned into reality.

One of the few luxuries Phree had purchased after the dust settled from the Mayflower discovery and her bank account had bulged, was a new car. Still steeped in her Midwest practical values, she went to the local Dodge showroom, picked out a fully loaded Caravan, and passed her old Honda on to a very happy Emily. Approaching her wonderful new car in the parking lot, she chuckled at the irony of owning such a kick-ass car while soon being able to walk to work every day from the caretaker's home at the back of the property. *I've got to come up with a name for my new home. I can't keep calling it the caretaker's home.*

A set of headlights came toward her as she slid behind the wheel of the minivan and started her car. *One of the girls must have forgotten something.* She squinted to see who it was, but the car's lights were so bright she swiveled her head away from the glare. As the car turned and parked rather close to her on the driver's side, she felt a cold dread trail down her spine, and panic settle in her thumping chest. Her ex-husband sneered at her through the windows.

Gary had parked so close that she couldn't get the car door open. Throwing her car into reverse, she backed out far enough so she could angle her car toward the long driveway where an escape could be made if necessary. She fought the urge to drive off, but she needed to know what the heck he was up to. He had never been physically violent toward her or Emily, so she calmed her breathing a bit and put on her I'm-in-control-and-feeling-bitchy face. She'd let him speak first. He swaggered toward her with an odd gait, and she figured he was holding a bottle of Jack behind his leg as he walked toward her.

Phree had once thought her 'Knight in Shining Armor' was going to save her from the loneliness and isolation she had felt growing up. He would stand by her and be her best friend for life while he protected their family with love and economic security. It was too late by the time she realized that she had married an adult male instead of a man. Their life was all about Gary, and all about his love of gambling. Going to 'the boats' was his preference, but her ex would gamble on anything, with anyone, at any time.

When she looked back on their years of marriage, Phree couldn't figure out why she hadn't left him a long time ago. Naïve? Young? Afraid? Or just plain stupid? Probably a combination of all those things intermingled with other excuses as well. In the end, she didn't have to make the decision. He grew a stupid soul patch on his chin because he thought it made him look cool and sexy, started a relationship with a young, busty cocktail waitress at one of the casinos, got her pregnant, and walked out on his teenage daughter and clueless wife. At the time, Phree was devastated, but divorce had been a liberating gift from The Bastard, as the Bunco group fondly called him.

Approaching the driver's side door, Gary twirled his hand at the wrist, making a roll-down-your-window motion. Phree pressed a button and dropped the window about three inches. He rested a hand on the top of the car door, leaned in, and said, "Well, well, look what Miss Richie Rich Important is driving these days." He swept his arm toward the old convent. "Must be nice to have so much money to waste on this rundown, piece-of-shit building. Someone told me you're going to sew in there. Is that true?"

Gary straightened and pushed a hand through disheveled hair. Phree could smell alcohol but chose to say nothing. She was thinking it might be time to bolt from this unfortunate scene, but she didn't want to leave him in this condition on her property. He had already ruined so many of her dreams; she was not going to give him free reign on this one.

Tilting his face close to the opening of the car window, he spat out, "Well? Is it true? Did you buy this whole rundown place just so you and that skanky group of friends you have could sew here?"

Phree finally spoke. "I think you should leave, Gary. This is private property, and you're not welcome here." She put the car in reverse and inched backwards, but Gary held tight to the window frame.

"Oh, I see how it is." He huffed out his chest trying to be indignant. "You're too good…too *wealthy* for me. Don't forget, Miss Important Mayflower Society," he teetered as he tried to stay upright, "I'm the father of your child."

The garbled words were slurred, and Phree wondered just how drunk he was. If the circumstances had been different, she probably would have laughed at the asinine way he was acting, but right now Phree was beginning to feel panic sneak into her consciousness. "Believe me, Gary, that's something that I wish I could forget."

"Well, the way I look at it, you should be sharing some of that money with me."

"And how did you figure that one out?" *Einstein.*

"I stayed with you for all those years." Wobble. "I was working and providing a home for you and my daughter, while you did nothing. On top of it all that Pilgrim crap was in *my* attic while I lived there."

"This is ludicrous on so many levels that I'm not even going to answer you, except to say, NO."

"I don't think you understand, bitch. I. NEED. MONEY. And I deserve half of what you got for that junk. Everyone thinks so."

"Who's everyone…you and your child bride? Or you and the dealers at the casino?"

Faster than she thought possible, he produced a wooden baseball bat that he had kept hidden behind his leg. He raised it to the hood of her car and shouted, "You bitch!" Spittle flew from his mouth and Phree stomped on the gas. The car was still in reverse, and it sped backwards just as Gary heaved the bat down. The club pounded the gravel, and dust and pebbles spewed from the impact.

"Get out of here!" Phree screamed. "I'm calling the police!"

"Go ahead! Call your asshole boyfriend, the big bad policeman. He doesn't scare me." Panting like a dog on hot day, he hurled the wooden bat toward the building. It circled end over end in a crazy spinning motion and fell far short of its intended target. Walking backwards a few steps, he shook his pointed finger at Phree. Near breathless, he said, "I need money, and I'm going to get my fair share from you."

Grasping her cell phone in her hand, Phree watched him stumble toward his rattletrap of a car. She moved her brand new minivan a long way backward, to give her ex enough room to back out of his space. She would be able to drive around him and speed away if she needed. But she could see he was spent. He had delivered his message.

Tears fell and her sobs grew while she watched the taillights grow smaller on his car as it wound its way down the meandering drive. It pissed her off that he was so delusional to actually think he was deserving of a portion of the Mayflower money. Bullying her had always been his way to get whatever he wanted from her, and he apparently hadn't figured out that she was not playing that game anymore. Gary was a bottomless pit when it came to needing money for gambling—he could never have enough. He was becoming more and more desperate and irrational, and it frightened her how he boldly drove while drunk.

One thing was for sure: The Bastard must owe someone a heck of a lot of money.

Chapter 13
May Bunco at Helen's

"I'm so glad we decided to change up the rotation of hosting duties when we were in Vegas," Nedra said. "Otherwise, you'd all be at my house for Bunco tonight."

"I was happy to draw May out of the hat, or should I more accurately say, the martini glass," Helen said. "Even though it's still a little chilly tonight, it's nice to host a warmer month and be able to serve drinks and appetizers on the patio." She held up a wine bottle in one hand and a crystal pitcher of ice water in the other. "Anyone?"

"I'm loving this virgin sangria," said Beth as she plunged a ladle into the ruby red liquid that filled the vintage punch bowl. "I really need to get this recipe."

"Phree made it up, and I copied it word for word from her the last time she made it for us. I'll e-mail it to you, but, as usual, you might have to remind me." As Helen topped off Nancy's wineglass, she said, "What's the news about Michael? We all know he moved into that fabulous log cabin home a few weeks ago, but haven't heard much about him since then."

"They're busy settling in." Nancy had recently reconnected with a boyfriend from her college days. After nearly twenty years, the spark was still there for both of them, and Michael Gibson had moved back to the Chicago area with his son after his wife had passed away. "Nick is spending a lot of time with his grandparents in the city, and I'm spending a lot of time at Casa Gibson." Nancy smiled. "We're all having a lot of fun."

"No need to dig any deeper," Marge said. "We get the picture."

Rosa patted Marge's hand and said, "Slow down, cowgirl. Some of us might want to do a little excavating on this one. Should we start planning a wedding shower yet?"

As always, Nancy flushed a bright red. "Maybe soon. Nothing definite." Nancy picked up an empty paper plate and fanned her rosy face. "I promise, you'll all be the first to know when, or should I say if, we decide to tie the knot."

"What do you mean *IF*?" Beth said. "We practically dragged you through a knothole kicking and screaming for the past ten months, until you finally realized he was crazy for you."

"I just don't want to jinx anything. I'm a little gun-shy at this point."

Helen could see Nancy squirming and said, "I can understand that feeling. Let's agree to no more marriage talk until Michael pops the question."

"I do love these Caprese tarts." Phree put two more on her plate. "I'm glad you made a bunch of them."

"So what happened after you called Brian about The Bastard's latest stunt?" Helen had been shocked by how foolish and scary Phree's ex had acted. "I still can't believe what he did."

"I'm having trouble taking it all in myself. I really feel bad for Emily. The emotional part of her thinks I should just give her father some money and everything would be okay. But the sensible part of her knows better. She's very torn." Phree poured a little more wine into her glass.

"What did my brother advise?" As a lawyer, Nedra's brother Brian had helped Phree with her divorce from The Bastard, as well as guiding her through the legalities of her recent discovery of Mayflower artifacts.

"The police filed a report that night, and then Brian filed a restraining order against Gary for both Emily and me. He told both of us to keep a record of any incidents with the creep. Well, he didn't actually call him a creep. I paraphrased a bit."

Marge wanted to know, "Can't more be done about what he did? He scared the crap out of you, and he could have seriously hurt you with that bat."

"It sucks, but at this point, no. It seems obvious to me that his distress is escalating—he's unhappy with his new wife and kids, and he's *very* desperate for money. I'm guessing his gambling is out of control again. But then again, when hasn't it been out of control?" She made a motorboat sound with her lips. "It terrifies me to think that he might approach Emily. She's so confused by all of this. I'm really glad for her sake that she's going far away to college in August. It's sad that I feel I need to keep her safe from him until she leaves."

"What about drunk driving? Can't they get him on that?"

"Yeah, they can, and I should have notified the police that night. I was pretty shook up, and didn't think of reporting it until I got home and settled down. That might be a good way to contain him if he gets nailed for a few DUI's. I'm scared to death he could hurt someone."

Crickets and tree frogs chorused in harmony as the big orange orb lowered itself in the west. Two of the women reached behind them for sweaters that were draped over the back of their chairs. It was only days till June, and the evenings were still quite chilly. Helen lit candles on the table and sidebar as darkness crept through the backyard. "I would have loved for Sunnie to have joined us tonight, but I can understand it was more important for her to stay home with Emily."

"I never would have left Emily alone at this point. We're both too afraid of what Gary might do. He knows better than to mess with Sunnie. She's always intimidated him." Scooping the last of the spinach-artichoke dip onto her plate, Phree said, "After I bought the retreat, Emily and I planned to postpone our trip to Plymouth and Duxbury until next year.

But I'm beginning to wonder if it wouldn't be a good idea to go this summer and get her out of here for a while."

"Between the retreat, The Bastard, Emily going away to college, and your mom hanging around, I'd say you've got your hands full, girlfriend," Nedra said.

"We're having a security system installed at home tomorrow, and we've already planned for security and surveillance at the retreat, but it will be a few weeks before they get to it at the MQR."

"What's the deal with your mom?" Nancy asked. "I've never known her to hang around this much."

"Good question." Phree blew out a long puff of air. "I have no idea. But all I can say is I was glad she was here the other night." Phree crossed and then rubbed her upper arms to warm them. "As much as it pains me to say it, I'm really enjoying her input at the MQR. She's come up with some great ideas. The sad thing is that I never trust Sunnie not to bolt at any given minute. I'm always waiting for something more important to call her away."

Helen noticed that no one had floated the Ricky question out to Rosa. *It's probably for the best. Let her enjoy a night with friends, without sad reminders.* She put a hand on Rosa's shoulder, leaned around her, and refilled her wineglass.

"How about you, Marge. Any grandbaby updates?"

"We're getting close to Niesha's due date. I'll be going to the baby shower in a few weeks." After 39 years, Marge had reconnected with a son she had given up for adoption when she was only sixteen years old. Jacob and his wife were due to have their first baby in about six weeks.

"On that note," Helen said, "I'll be right back." She set down the bottle of wine from which she had been pouring and headed to her sewing studio in the garage.

Beth rubbed her hands together. "Ooooo, I can't wait to see it!"

After much discussion, the women had made a baby quilt for Marge's grandchild, a boy to be named David. Helen had volunteered to quilt it on her new long-arm quilting machine, and they planned to send it to the shower with Marge. Helen approached with a neatly folded blue bundle. She positioned herself in front of all the women, held the two top corners, and spread her arms wide. "Ta-da!"

There were shrieks of approval, several woo-hoos, and some applause. Marge, the grandma-to-be, held her hands over her mouth.

"I take it you approve?" Helen asked.

"It's fabulous."

The friends moved in for a closer look.

Lettie had made a detailed drawing of a rocking horse and had it professionally printed on fabric. Nancy had used her skills and her new software to design a quilt around the hand-drawn panel. A Sunday had been scheduled for the all-day sewing session at Lettie's fiber arts studio, where each woman took part in piecing together the quilt. Helen brought the quilt top home, added the backing and batting, and then custom quilted it on her long-arm machine. Nedra had offered to hand stitch the binding.

"Aren't we quite the team?" Rosa said.

"Phree, I bet you could sell these patterns and panels at the MQR," Beth said, and looked toward Nedra. "Maybe you could use a photo of this in some of the social media sites."

"Great idea. I'll shoot it after I get the binding on."

Helen refolded the quilt. "I'll put this inside by the jackets, Ned. It's all yours for the last step."

"I have another gift for that little babe," Lettie said. "I'm having the original drawing of the rocking horse framed. As a matter of fact, it's at the framer's right now, otherwise I would have brought it with me tonight. Marge can add it to our group gift, and it can hang in the baby's room to complement the quilt we all made for David."

"Wow! What a perfect gift," Beth said. "That's a great idea, Lettie."

For the second time that evening, Marge's hands flew to cover her mouth. When she recovered from the surprise, she said, "I…I'm speechless. That's so generous. Thank you."

Excitement about the gifts and the birth of the group's first grandchild eventually turned back to casual conversation. Another wine bottle was emptied, and two more women reached for their sweaters. Someone asked Phree if she was still able to see Bill with all that was going on at the MQR plus her mother staying with her.

"Sunnie figured out what was going on in about three seconds. I swear that woman has her radar set so high she could be mistaken for a mind reader," Phree said. "But, yeah, Bill and I are still seeing each other. Neither of us wants to take this on the fast track. We're just enjoying each other's occasional company."

"Could you be any more vague?" Rosa said.

"Trust me…like you said between the MQR, my mom, Emily, and don't forget the chaos from The Bastard, there's really not a lot of time for even meals and sleeping, no less a romantic rendezvous."

"Well, what I want to know," Nancy looked toward Marge, "is what did Bud think about you quitting your job to become the GM at the quilters retreat?"

"You know my hubby—he's 100% behind me. He gets that this is an opportunity that will most likely never happen again, and he knows how much I want to do this." Marge smiled at Phree. "It's amazing. I feel so fortunate. I still can't believe this is happening." Unable to contain the excitement, she rubbed her hands together like a little girl. "I'm giving my two-week notice this Friday."

"If ever there was a perfect person for a job," Lettie said, "this is it. Phree will be lucky to have you."

Phree raised her wineglass. "Amen to that."

Marge stood and picked up the remains of a plated appetizer. "Many hands make light work, ladies. Let's help Helen get her patio cleared, and we can start playing Bunco."

Behind her back, Helen saluted Marge, the Sarge, as the women stifled giggles.

Chapter 14
Phree

It was Emily's Big Day—high school graduation.

From her vantage point near the top of the bleachers at Whitney High, Phree spotted The Bastard slipping through the door twenty minutes after "Pomp and Circumstance" had ended. Nudging first Sunnie on her left and then Nedra on her right, she pointed her chin toward her ex, and whispered, "Look who's finally here." She was happy to see him *only* for Emily's sake. "I'm glad he didn't drag wifey and their two little kids with him."

Not wanting the day to be any more uncomfortable than it was probably already going to be, Phree had opted not to invite her friend Bill to join them. Always the gentleman, and oh so different from The Bastard, Bill had understood. No muss, no fuss with this guy.

From high on her perch, Phree had watched as Emily walked in time with the music and took her seat among the assembly of graduates. Her head pivoted from door to door watching for her father to enter the over-warm gymnasium. About ten minutes into the event, Phree noticed that her daughter had stopped looking; she had given up. But Phree knew that after the ceremony, Gary would lie (as usual) and tell his child that he had been here from the beginning. Hadn't she seen him wave to her as she walked down the aisle with her partner? *Lying bastard.*

The creep hadn't shown up for Emily's Senior Honors Banquet, and while she tried to act as though it didn't bother her, their daughter had been hurt by his absence. Thank God Sunnie was stepping up to the plate by playing the role of grandmother to perfection. Accessory shopping for graduation had been on their agenda two days ago, along with a mani-pedi for each of them, and a fancy afternoon tea complete with scones and cucumber sandwiches. Feeling a rare rush of warmth toward her mother, Phree reached over and clasped Sunnie's hand. "Thanks for making this a special day for Emily."

Phree was surprised to find that her mother's eyes were shiny with moisture as she turned to look at her. "It was completely my pleasure." She smiled and dabbed her eyes with a ready tissue. "This is a big day. I'm so proud of both of you."

Parents and family members mingled with the graduates as last photos were snapped with classmates. Families posed together with their new Whitney High alumni while they were still decked out in the school's traditional red cap and gown. Marge and family were there for Val, and eventually the two friends met up for a photo op. Before the families went their own ways, Marge suggested a group picture. They handed their cameras to the Dean of Students, who was making the rounds among the graduates, and the large group snugged in together for the shot. Emily and Val were front and center with broad smiles and excited thoughts for their futures.

Rather than join in, Gary lingered off to the side, checking his watch. At one point, Phree tried to coax him to join in for the group picture, but he declined. "I'd just like one with Em and me." By this time, Phree had used so much self-control that a powerful headache was building up from grinding her teeth too much.

"Of course," she said politely for Emily's sake. "That will be a nice memento."

Gary grudgingly shuffled toward his child of eighteen years and stood by her side, not touching—not even shoulders, no hand slipped around her waist or fatherly peck on the cheek. Stock still and soldier straight—wishing to be anywhere but here. Phree was about to tell them to act like they knew each other, and then thought, "Screw it." She clicked the camera three times. They looked more like smiling acquaintances than a loving father and daughter. How very sad for Emily.

As the gym started to clear out, Phree asked, "You ready to leave, honey?"

"Yeah, I'm starving. Did you make reservations? Can Dad come with?"

Awkward.

"Of course he can." Big fake smile.

Gary obviously hadn't counted on this. "Well…I…that is…"

"Come on, Dad." Emily whined. "I never get to see you."

Gary gave his ex-wife a cutting look that would have once made her feel like a horrible person, someone in need of begging for her husband's forgiveness. She knew he was thinking of the restraining order against him, which Emily had conveniently forgotten about. "It's fine," Phree said, and decided not to cover for his sorry ass this time by trying to sugarcoat the difficult situation. "I've cleared it with Brian. You can have dinner with us." Emily looked at the ground, and this time The Bastard appeared as though he might explode. A fury of anger and blame burned from his eyes and was directed squarely at Phree. She smirked. *Gottcha*. But she instantly felt bad for her daughter, who right now looked like a sad and lonely little girl.

Phree's headache did *not* get any better during the tension-filled meal. Gary tried to upset her by ordering a top-of-the-line double bourbon which he pounded down before they had placed their dinner order. He motioned to the waitperson and ordered two more of the same, and in a voice that made it clear she would cause trouble, Phree told the embarrassed server, "Do *not* bring those drinks to this table."

Gary tried to get even by ordering six appetizers for the four of them, and then proceeding to request the most expensive meal on the menu along with several side dishes that he didn't bother to touch. "Guess I'm not as hungry as I thought I was." He laughed too loudly as he patted his stomach.

Happy to finally be getting out of the crowded restaurant, Phree dangled the keys to the new minivan in front of Emily as they walked outside. Her daughter grabbed at them so fast that they flew out of her hand and skittered through the parking lot. Giggling, Emily dashed after them, but not before calling over her shoulder, "Sorry, Mom."

While Emily was retrieving the wayward car keys, Phree turned to Sunnie. "How the hell did this get so out of hand today?"

"That doesn't matter, honey. What matters is how you handled it, and from what I could tell you used up a mountain of patience on that jerk today. But, in the bigger picture, you did the right thing for your daughter."

Pulling out of the restaurant's driveway, Emily announced, "Dad told me that his house has been foreclosed on." Phree closed her eyes while pinching the bridge of her nose. "He said he doesn't know what will happen to them or where they'll go."

Phree chose not to comment.

"Well?" Emily sounded impatient.

"Well, what? What do you expect *me* to do?"

"Maybe help them out."

"Emily, we've had this talk several times. It's not going to happen."

"But why? Why can't you give them just enough so they can stay in their house?"

Gary's infidelity had become known to Phree when his young girlfriend with the swollen belly surfaced, and divorce was what all the adults had agreed upon. Even with Phree's years of diligent bill paying by scraping together enough to keep the Clarke family afloat through years of Gary's job-hopping and gambling debts, they each left the marriage with tainted credit scores. Phree's numbers slowly got better over the years, until they finally skyrocketed with the Mayflower discovery. Before Gary's credit hit rock bottom, he had managed to purchase a small home for his pregnant bride that the bank had taken back from its previous owners.

"Why won't I give them money? Seriously, Em, because your father and his new family are not my problem, that's why. And I'm not going to change my mind." She was sure Gary had asked their daughter to solicit money for him. "So, tell him you asked me, and that I, the big bad person that I am, said no again."

Emily's shoulders sagged as she checked both ways before making a left turn. Exhaling a long breath, she said, "I know, Mom. You're right. I'm sorry."

Sunnie had remained neutral on the topic of Gary throughout the day, and Phree was grateful when her mother changed the subject from the backseat. "Now that you've gotten your diploma, honey, what are your plans for the summer?"

Emily chatted with her grandmother about lifeguarding at the pool this summer, getting ready for college, and how she couldn't wait to leave Whitney. Supporting her throbbing cranium on the headrest, Phree closed her eyes. With graduation over, if she was lucky, she wouldn't have to see or hear from The Bastard for a long, long time.

Chapter 15
Rosa

The office at The Pizza Depot felt confining and claustrophobic to Rosa. What she used to think of as her 'little cocoon' that kept her insulated from the outside world and customers had begun to close in on her. Not even the freshly painted, buttery yellow walls could cheer her anymore. She needed a window, or some fresh air, or some good news.

Terry poked his head into the room. "Hey babe, would you like a sandwich? I'm going to have an Italian beef for lunch." He smiled. "I'm buying."

"Could you make me three Italian Beefs? I'll be done here in a few minutes, and I think I'm going to head over to see Phree at the retreat." Rosa stapled a paid receipt to its invoice and slipped it into the folder marked June. "I'll surprise her and Sunnie with hot sandwiches."

Terry went from a smile to a wide, hopeful grin. Rosa knew he was happy that she was spontaneously visiting someone instead of going home and hiding from the world. "You got it," he said. "Would you like fries with that, ma'am?"

Between the sounds of pounding hammers, electric drills, and the whine of circular saws, Phree put her hands to her cheeks and said, "I could kiss you!" as Rosa showed up in the entryway of the MQR with The Pizza Depot bag. "I can tell by the glorious smell coming from that bag that you have those incredible world famous Italian beefs that I love so much."

Rosa grinned at Phree's reaction. "I don't know about the 'world famous' comment, but I've got one for Sunnie, too, if she's here."

"She's here, but shhh, don't tell her about the sandwiches. I'll be happy to eat hers, too."

"Well, the good news is my hubby made four—'just in case,' he said."

"Ooooo." Phree faked biting on her knuckles. "Looks like I'm going to have to kiss him, too. Sunnie, come quick!"

Wiping her hands on a rag, Sunnie came out from the Hannah Brewster Dry Goods room where quilt supplies would be for sale once the retreat opened. Pointing back at the room, she said, "I was right in there, Phree. I heard every word that you said, and there's no way you're going to eat my sandwich." Sunnie connected her arm with Rosa's and placed a gentle kiss on her cheek. "How ya doing today, girlie?"

"Right now I'm hungry."

"Let's go to the dining room and dig in," Phree said. "I'll catch you up with what's going on around here."

"It looks to me like you've made a ton of progress since the other night when we were all here." Rosa stepped aside as two workmen carried in an oversized window and placed it next to a large hole in the outside wall where it would soon be installed.

"We've got a great crew. They're dedicated and committed to finishing on time. Oh, and did I mention they're creative too?"

"I'll get something to wipe down this table," Sunnie said and headed toward the kitchen. Two of the tables acted as the headquarters for the construction crews, with stacks of papers and blueprints covering their surfaces. One was kept clutter-free for lunches and meetings, and the fourth was pushed up against a wall for the landscape architect and interior designer to share.

"What brings you here today, kiddo?"

"I have an idea for the retreat I wanted to share. But mostly I just want to stay busy today."

Phree gave her a knowing smile and reached for her friend's hand. "June 5th. His fifteenth birthday is today, huh? Well, you're welcome to hang out here for as long as you want. There's plenty to do around this place to keep a hundred people busy."

"Thanks, Phree. When I leave here, I plan to go back to The Depot and wait tables until I can drop into bed and fall asleep without thinking…or remembering."

All three women unwrapped their 'world famous' Italian beef sandwiches at the same time. The gold foil-backed waxed paper wrapping kept the sandwiches steamy warm. "Fries?" Rosa asked. "I'll just put them in the middle of the table. I think Terry made an extra-large batch for us."

Phree closed her eyes and whimpered, "Mmmmm," as she took her first bite. Au jus dripped down her chin. Dabbing with a paper napkin, she added, "I'm in food heaven. I just love these things."

"While my daughter is busy putting herself into a coma over there, tell me your idea for the retreat."

As usual, Rosa really had no appetite, but she was nibbling a small bite here and there to make it appear as though she were eating. "Well, for the rooms upstairs where the guests will sleep, I was thinking that instead of simply using numbers to identify the rooms, they could be named after quilt blocks with a plaque of some kind. Like Churn Dash, Ohio Star, Dresden Plate, Log Cabin…you get the idea. And then I thought that all of us could help make little six-inch blocks to match with the names. We could have them framed and hang them, well probably secure them somehow, next to the appropriate rooms."

Phree's eyes grew as she swallowed an extra-large mouthful of the beef sandwich. She gulped in a sharp breath of air and said, "Genius! I love it, Rosa. It's absolutely perfect. Would you be willing to organize the project?"

"Yeah, I think I'd like to do that." Rosa felt a smidge of panic bloom in her chest, so she added a disclaimer. "If I can't…I mean…I'm afraid…"

"Take a deep breath," Sunnie said.

After a slow intake of air, she finished, "I'm sure Marge or one of the others would take over if I can't finish for some reason."

"No worries, hon. I'd be happy to work on this project with you, if you'd like," Sunnie said. "Let me know a time or day that's good for you, and we'll get the ball rolling."

Rosa gave her head an enthusiastic bob. She couldn't speak past the lump of relief that had settled in her throat. Phree was right; Sunnie might just be a mind reader after all.

"Anyone want to split the last sandwich?" Phree asked.

Rosa shook her head, and Sunnie said, "It's all yours."

Taking the opportunity to change the subject, Rosa said, "Will you be staying for a while to help Phree?"

Sunnie instantly looked uncomfortable and gave Rosa a weak smile. "I'm hoping to be around for a while. That is, if Phree will have me."

Rosa observed an eye-roll from Phree as she started her second sandwich. Ignoring her friend's annoyance, Rosa asked Sunnie, "What's going on at City Care? I'm surprised you've been able to get away for so long."

"Right now I've got these two kids I'm trying desperately to help. Shark and …"

"Sorry to interrupt." Josh's voice boomed off the walls as he walked into the dining room. "Can you come take a look at this, Phree? We need your opinion."

Phree stood. "Sure thing. Sorry, ladies, I'll be right back. No one better eat my sandwich while I'm gone."

"So, anyway," Sunnie said, "It's really more of the same at City Care. I'm trying to plug these young guys into odd jobs around the complex for a while to keep them off the streets. I've offered them food and beds in exchange for their help. So far it's working out great for all of us."

Again, Rosa couldn't speak. The lump in her throat had swelled to a bulge as she closed her eyes and prayed someone like Sunnie was looking after her son. She felt the warmth of a caring hand on hers. "Hang in there, Rosa. You'll get him back."

Rosa tied on her Pizza Depot apron and loaded up the large pouch-like pockets with the usual waitress paraphernalia: straws, order pad, pens, and a few spare beverage napkins.

"You know you don't have to do this," Terry said. "You already look exhausted."

"That's the idea. I basically want to work until I can go home and pass out." An unsteady smile crossed her face. "Besides, we've always celebrated the boys' birthdays at The Depot, so we could be together while you worked. There's something comforting about being here with you." She leaned in to her husband for an embrace. His man smell mingled with the scent of pizza spices and brought her a sense of safe familiarity.

By 7:00 p.m., Terry suggested his exhausted wife take a short break. "There's a booking for nine at table seventeen. When they get here, I'll have Jenny get them started. Whenever you feel like it, come back on the floor and take over."

Rosa had been happily distracted by a dining room full of customers, and as she had hoped, was already dead on her feet. A few minutes in the breakroom with her shoes off and feet propped on a chair would feel heavenly. The moment her thoughts swung back to her son, she pulled one foot and then the other off the chair. Stuffing the swollen appendages back into her walking shoes, she loosened the laces and tied them. It had only been about fifteen minutes, but she felt somewhat recharged.

Terry passed her in the hallway, and she asked, "Where do you want me to start?"

"Seventeen is here and seated. Can you start there so Jenny can take her break?"

"Got it." Halfway through the dining room, on her way to table seventeen, she stopped and stood stock still. Sitting at the double-wide table were all her friends from the Bunco Club along with Sunnie. Terry came up behind her, untied her apron, and removed it from her waist. With slight pressure on the small of her back, he urged her forward. She approached the table with small, tentative steps. All the women had smiles and were looking at her. In the center of the table was a sheet cake. It read, 'Happy Birthday, Ricky. We love you and miss you.'

Lettie stood and guided her best friend into a seat. "His birthday needs to be celebrated. We didn't want you to be alone tonight."

Chapter 16
Phree

"I have to hand it to you, Sunnie, that was a great last-minute idea getting everyone over to The Depot tonight. At first I thought Rosa was going to bolt out of there, but by the end of the evening, I think she actually had a good time."

"She shouldn't always try to hold everything in. It's impossible to do, and the results are counterproductive." Sunnie topped off their wineglasses and then rested her feet on the coffee table across from Phree's. "Ah, that feels good. I'm glad Emily was sleeping over at Shelley's tonight, otherwise, I would have stayed home with her. I don't like how irrational your charming ex-husband's been acting."

"I would have had her come with—even if she chose to sit in a booth by herself and pout all night." Phree placed a sofa pillow behind her head and leaned back. "I could see her doing that."

"Like mother, like daughter," Sunnie scoffed.

"Yeah, you're probably right." Several moments passed, then Phree asked, "Do you think he could hurt his own daughter? Gary, I mean. He's never been violent or used force of any kind on either of us, but he really scared me the other night. I mean a baseball bat. Seriously? What was he thinking?"

"I guess if we aren't sure, it's better to play it safe. He certainly has quite a story built up in his mind about deserving some of your Mayflower money."

"For just a nanosecond, I thought about giving him some. If you can believe it, I actually felt sorry for Tiffany and their kids. But we both know that Miss Homewrecker and her children would never see a cent, and he'd be broke again in weeks."

"You've got a good heart, Phree. You always have. But you might as well go to a casino and bet it all on red, or black, or whatever they do in those places." Sunnie muffled a yawn. "Because you know that's what Gary will do with *any* money he gets."

"I suppose you're right. But I guess I could pay his mortgage directly to the lender, and not give him any cash. That way he wouldn't be able to gamble it away."

"At least not until he went to the bank and remortgaged his home behind his missy's back."

"Good point. I never thought about that. We'll just have to keep a watchful eye on Emily until she's gone to college."

In the quiet of the room, June bugs could be heard as they thumped against the window screens. They would lay on their backs, legs wiggling and squirming until they righted themselves and flew off.

"I need a good name for the caretaker's house. I can't keep calling it the caretaker's house," Phree said. "It makes it seem as though I'm not committed or connected to the retreat…like I'm just biding my time in someone else's home. It's going to be my home soon, and I'd like to name it something appropriate. Any ideas?"

"I'll have to think about it. You're looking for something to do with the Mayflower or pilgrims, right?"

"Yeah. I had thought about the second ship to arrive a year after the Mayflower. It was called the Fortune. But to call your home 'The Fortune' might sound a little pretentious and a lot braggy to people who don't know the facts about the names of the ships.

"How about the Compact? Or the Cottage?"

"I like the sound of the Cottage, but it still doesn't seem quite right. I'd rather it be a more direct tie-in with the

Mayflower. Like the names we're giving the rooms in the retreat."

"I know you decided the kitchen will be called the Galley. What are some other parts of an old time ship? Captain's Quarters, the Hold, the Bridge, Steerage, Crow's Nest?" Sunnie started laughing and couldn't get her next words out.

"What? What's so funny?" Phree had no idea why her mother was in hysterics, but it was contagious and she started laughing right along with Sunnie.

After several attempts at speaking, wiping tears from her eyes, and snort-laughing like a little pig, Sunnie managed to say, "Poop Deck! How about calling it the Poop Deck?"

Mother and daughter howled until finally their laughter trailed off to sniffles and smiles. "Well, that felt good," Sunnie said. "Sorry about that. I guess I was being immature and not much help."

Aside from the fact that Phree realized she hadn't shared a good laugh with her mom in years, she waved off Sunnie's apology. "No, you were great. You gave me some good ideas to springboard from. What do you think of calling the GM's office the Bridge? That's the heart of the ship—the point where the ship is commanded. Or, in our case, the office from where the Mayflower Quilters Retreat will be run."

"And don't forget it will be commandeered by none other than the Sarge." Sunnie started giggling again. "Maybe she should be promoted to Captain."

"Excellent idea. Let's get her a plaque for her desk to go along with the ones we'll have above the doors to the rooms. ...Captain Marge Russell. I like it," Phree said. "Okay, my house...drumroll please..." Sunnie drummed her index fingers on the table to help with the announcement. "The Crow's Nest! I think it's perfect because I'll always be looking out over the retreat."

Sunnie applauded. "Bravo, the Crow's Nest it is."

"And..." Phree paused and put both of her hands up, calling for silence. "Let's get plaques for all the washrooms that say Poop Deck!"

Both women doubled over, wailing with laughter. How good it felt to enjoy some simple silliness together.

"So, back to my question. What are you going to do with this house after you move to the Crow's Nest?"

"I plan to sell it. I thought of renting it, but I don't want the headache of dealing with all the crap that goes with that." Phree's antennae went up—maybe she was more like her mom than she thought. She tilted her head to one side and took a long look at her mother. "Why?"

Sunnie hesitated. "I've been thinking..." She swirled her wineglass and studied the spinning liquid as though the secret to happiness was about to be revealed in the mini-whirlpool.

Phree wasn't sure she liked where this was heading. "...And?"

"There's no easy way to say this."

Overreacting, Phree jerked her feet off the coffee table, and a magazine slid to the floor. "I know, I know, you've got to leave tomorrow and won't be back." She glared at Sunnie. "Just say it. I've known all along this was too good to be true, and something like this was going to happen, so it's not a surprise. I'm not even upset." Tears were about to betray her last statement. She stood and turned so her mother wouldn't see their flow. They had just shared such a fun time together, and now this...The Famous Sunnie Eaton Disappearing Act. "Emily is so happy you've been here...been like a real grandmother to her after all these years." Phree didn't care if she hurt Sunnie's feelings. *Good, I hope that hit home.*

"No. No. That's not it at all. Come. Sit down. Let me tell you what I'd like to do."

Phree took an extra moment to calm down. They had just enjoyed such a rare fun moment, laughing and bonding, and now Sunnie was about to destroy the whole evening with some lame excuse. Phree plopped heavily onto the sofa, arms folded, and lips pressed tight.

Sunnie laughed, "That's exactly what you used to do when you were a little girl and got mad at me. Flop down somewhere and pout."

"I'm not pouting. I'm pissed. There's a difference."

"Why the heck are you so pissed? I said three words, 'I've been thinking,' and you jump to some crazy conclusion."

Phree covered her face with her hands, blew out a long stretch of air, and said, "Can we just get to the point?" She uncovered her face and slammed her hands in her lap. "What is it?"

"This isn't how I wanted this to go." Now it was Sunnie's turn to yank her feet from the coffee table. "Let's skip the whole thing. Never mind."

"No. I want to know—I'm dying to know. I'm begging you to tell me."

Sunnie's eyes darted around the room, and Phree thought her mother might start crying. *I am such a scumbag.* "I'm sorry. It's been a long couple of days. Let's start this conversation over."

It was Sunnie's turn to cross her arms over her chest and glare at her daughter through squinted eyes. Mother and daughter were at their usual standoff, but this time it didn't last long, as Sunnie said, "Why does it always have to come down to an argument with you? Can we ever get past your anger and disappointment with me as a mother and simply have a healthy relationship?"

"How can we do that when you constantly run back to City Care every time someone needs you to fix a hangnail or something equally trivial?" Phree exhaled through her nose and let her shoulders slump. "I'm sorry. That wasn't fair. I'm acting like a spoiled child."

"You know, Phree, I'm not the only mother in the world that worked. I realize you feel as though I've let you down your whole life. I don't know how to make it better, but I *have* been trying." Sunnie gulped the remainder of her wine. She tipped the bottle to her glass, and red liquid flowed quickly to the brim. She thumped the near-empty bottle onto the coffee table, looked at her daughter, and said, "I tendered my resignation at CCC last week."

Phree felt her eyes grow wide.

"I want to live down here and work with you at the retreat. I think we'd make a good team."

As her head sagged forward and her mouth dropped open, Phree couldn't get a word past her dry-as-a-bone throat. Moments later, when she could squeak out a few words, she said, "I…I…I'm shocked."

"I can see that." Sunnie held the wine bottle out toward her daughter. "Would you like to finish this off?"

Without speaking, Phree took the bottle, tilted it to her mouth, closed her eyes, took two gulps to empty its contents, and then slumped back on the sofa. "Thanks. I definitely needed that."

"I take it this is not particularly good news to you?" Sunnie was expressionless, and Phree could not get a read on her mother's thoughts or feelings.

"No, it's not that...but resigning from City Care? I never thought I'd ever hear those words come out of your mouth. What happened? Why? You love that place. It's your life."

Sunnie stood, walked around the coffee table, and sat next to her daughter. She picked up one of Phree's hands with both of hers. "You're right. I do love what Wolf and I built at City Care Chicago. I feel we all had a good life there, and I'm proud that we helped a lot of people. But, with your father gone, City Care doesn't seem right anymore. It's hard to explain—I feel empty there."

Phree felt her mother increase the grip on her hands, holding on for support.

"But you're wrong about one thing, Phreedom. CCC is not my life. It may surprise you, but you and Emily are my life." Sunnie smiled, and Phree saw love in her mother's eyes. "I've always loved you more than you ever realized. And I love Emily just as much." Reaching up and stroking Phree's cheek, she asked, "Do you think it's possible we could start over and heal our broken relationship?"

The pure look of love she witnessed from her mother permitted Phree to lower years of built-up barriers and allow hope to sneak into her heart again. "Yes," she croaked, almost too softly to hear. "Yes," she smiled, and said a little louder as happy tears rimmed her eyes.

Sunnie embraced her daughter and whispered every mother's lament into Phree's hair, "Forgive me for any pain I might have caused you. It's hard being a mother, and I did the best job that I could."

Chapter 17
Rosa

"I only wondered what he did yesterday. That's all." Rosa was being defensive. She threw her hands in the air and let them flop to her side, as though she was befuddled by her oldest son's response. "For crying out loud, it was his fifteenth birthday. He's my child. I'm worried about him. I only wondered if he thought about me—about us."

"Mom, I've been awake for a total of a half an hour, and you've asked that question four times already. We're all worried about him, but we *have* to keep living."

"That seems rather heartless, Alex."

"Oh, really? Do you think if you ask that question 50 or 100 times that he'll walk through the door, or that I'll finally be able to give you the answer you want to hear? What good does it do to ask it over and over and over again?"

Rosa felt tears bubbling to the surface of her currently dry eyes. "What's your problem, anyway?"

"Do you think because we went to a ball game a few weeks ago that you're off the hook for being my mother?"

"I thought we had a great time that day." Rosa was stunned. "Why are you being so mean?"

"We did have a nice day—that's the point."

Running a hand over his stubbly face, her son said, "I don't know. I'm sorry, Mom. I guess I wish that once in a while you'd ask me what I did yesterday, or today, or last week. I just wanted to share something, but nothing ever seems important when pitted against all the intense grief over Ricky. Do you even care that I'm home for the summer?"

Rosa had one child that was missing, and she truly didn't want her other one to mentally check out of the family. "I'm sorry, honey. I get so focused on Ricky that I forget about everything and everyone else. Please believe it's not because I love you less—it's me...not you." Rosa sat across from her son at the breakfast table, and after drying her eyes with a tissue, she smiled at him. "Can we start over? What's your news, honey?"

"Well, it's not exactly news, but I've decided on a roommate for next year at school, and they've already rented an apartment off campus."

"Great. I'd say that's good news. You wanted to live off campus for your last year, and I think it's a perfect idea. You'll get a feel for what it's like to be on your own, and the experience will prepare you for graduate school. What's your roommate's name? Do I know him?"

"Well, actually the two of you have already met."

Rosa felt her smile wilt as she detected there was more to this story. "...And?"

"It's Jenny, Mom."

"As in Jenny Carlson? Your girlfriend?" Rosa's voice went up a notch. She liked Jenny; Alex had been dating her for almost two years. Rosa remained calm, but she didn't feel all that calm inside.

"Yeah. I've been kind of afraid to tell you, but Dad said to talk..."

"Dad? Dad knows?" She had always been the go-to parent, the one on the front line when it came to the kids. This simple statement showed her how far she had slipped from her duties as mother. Her 'mom radar' was usually set very high, and it surprised her that her antennae hadn't even picked up a blip about Alex's new living arrangement.

Red cheeked, Alex looked embarrassed. "Well, I wasn't sure how you'd take it, and I didn't want to upset you any more than you already are...over Ricky, that is."

So many scenarios were running through her head, and Rosa didn't want to alienate her son any more than she evidently already had. Alex would turn twenty-one in October, and Jenny had celebrated her twentieth birthday when the Bunco girls were in Vegas. Age-wise they were both legal to choose to live together. But with her mother's eyes, she could see just how much could go wrong. "So what did Dad say?"

"He says he's fine with it if you are."

Arrrgh—in other words, he was leaving her to be the bad person by putting up a stink if she didn't approve. "Oh, honey..."

"Mom, we're talking about getting married after I graduate anyway. If that helps at all."

"What about grad school?"

"I don't think we'd be the first married couple in grad school."

"What if she gets pregnant?"

"Then you'll be a grandmother, and I'll be a father."

The truth was that Terry and she had 'shacked up' (as they called it back then) for a few months before they got married, but they had never shared that information with the kids. *Maybe it's best for them to find out if they're compatible or not before they get married.* But when she looked at him, her mother's eyes still saw a little baby boy. He was obviously going to do this with or without her blessing. *I can't lose another son...not over this.* "Please promise me she won't get pregnant before you get married."

Alex smiled. "I guarantee it, Mom."

But Rosa was chilled by his assurance.

Chapter 18
Phree

A hint of summer humidity along with the thick scent of lilacs drifted on the morning air as Phree took the chair across from Sunnie at the kitchen table. Last night had been an exhausting emotional breakthrough for the two women, and Phree was glad they had decided to further discuss her mother's bombshell announcement the next morning. After the usual pleasantries of 'how did you sleep,' and 'it looks like it's going to be a beautiful day,' Phree said, "Emily won't be home from Shelley's until this afternoon, and we've got some time before we have to get to the retreat. Tell me what you're thinking. How do you see this working?"

"I think it best if I explain what I would ideally like to see happen. After that, we can whittle it down to whatever you're comfortable with."

Phree nodded her head. "That sounds like a good plan." She had wanted a close mother/daughter relationship for as long as she could remember, and while half of her was cautious and guarded, the other half held out for one more try.

"As I told you last night, I'll be leaving City Care. The time frame for that to happen is fluid, depending on what we decide today. Since I've been spending so much time here, I've already cut back most of my responsibilities and handed over many of my duties to Dan and his wife, Mary. There are three families that have wanted to have more permanent participation in the community, and I'll suggest this might be a good time to embrace them as members. We have plenty of room in the complex, and of course, my apartment will also now be available. I'm afraid City Care Chicago needs a shot of fresh blood to keep it viable."

Phree was surprised when she felt a tiny pang of sorrow that their family home would soon belong to someone else. "That must have been a tough decision to make."

"I admit that I was in denial since your father died. I thought I could handle the responsibilities with the same passion that Wolf and I had for all those years. I'm almost ashamed to confess that my commitment died with Wolf." Sunnie steepled her fingers in front of her mouth, as though she was saying a prayer. "I've wanted out for a long time. I simply didn't know what I'd do with myself. Until now."

"Give me your vision of how this will work. Is that why you wanted to know what I was doing with the house? Would you like to live here?"

Sunnie fluttered her hands in front of her as she shook her head. "Oh, my, no! This house is way too big for me. I guess I was just being nosey. Making small talk is all." Sunnie scooted up toward the edge of her chair, arms crossed in front of her resting on the kitchen table. "We've already discussed that I could teach some classes occasionally. What I'd also like to do..." She uncrossed her arms and then folded her hands together, squeezing them tightly.

Phree sensed that her mother was *very* nervous and reached across the table, resting her own hand over Sunnie's. "Take a breath, Mom." She rarely called Sunnie "Mom" but it seemed like they both might need it right now. "Go on, you're doing fine."

Sunnie relaxed and smiled at her. "I love it when you call me Mom. Maybe that's something we can work toward."

Phree nodded in agreement, "I'd like that, too."

"Okay this is it. Marge will be your GM, but she can't be there 24/7. She'll need to be home with her family at night, and she'll also need days off. I thought that I could be her assistant of sorts and take over when she's not there. You know I'm qualified to run an organization of this size—I've been doing it for most of my adult life." Sunnie was picking up steam and her enthusiasm was touching to Phree. "I'm not a nurse like Marge, but I certainly have knowledge of how to handle simple medical emergencies and at the very least keep from panicking. I can fill in wherever you might need me on any given day."

Phree had a moment of dread, but asked the question without voicing any distress. "Are you thinking of maybe living in the Crow's Nest with me?"

"Oh, heavens no. We'd kill each other!" Sunnie clasped both of her hands over her mouth, and her eyes grew wide. She looked like a guilty little girl. "Sorry, I didn't mean..."

Phree laughed, "You're right—how very true. We would probably kill each other."

Sunnie removed her hands and said, "Whew. Thought for a second there I might have put my foot in it. But, no, living with you never crossed my mind. What I *am* thinking is that I could live in one of the suites upstairs. I'd be on site all night if I was needed, and I could triage problems. I'd only call you or Marge if it was a dire emergency." Scooting back in her chair all the way, Sunnie nodded once to signify 'that's all I got' and punctuated her finale with a broad smile.

"I love it. I can't find any way that this is not a great idea. Which suite would you like?"

"I'll take whichever one you're okay with." Sunnie clasped her hands together. "I haven't been this excited in years. I'm happy you believe in me, and want me to share in the retreat with you."

As Phree stood to embrace Sunnie, she checked the digital clock on the microwave. "You're very welcome, and I'm excited, too. But *I* should be thanking *you*. This is a perfect idea, and having your knowledge and creativity on board will be priceless for the MQR. Besides that," Phree held her mom at arm's length, "I'm looking forward to building the retreat with my mother by my side."

Sunnie started to fuss and clear away the coffee cups and remnants left from their morning oatmeal. "I'll contact City Care and make my resignation effective on a mutual date."

Phree thought to herself, "This will be the ultimate test. We're going to finally bridge our differences and live happily ever after—or we truly are going to kill each other."

Chapter 19
Sunnie

"To answer your question, I've only got one thing that I'd really like to tie up before I leave City Care. I've got these two kids I've been working with and counseling a little, I think I told you about them: Shark and Cardo. I'd like to make sure that they transition a little more before I leave them."

Phree spun around and said a little too loudly, "What did you say?"

"I…uh…just thought that…well, there would be enough time before I moved in. I don't have to…I can hand them over to Dan, if it's going to upset you." Sunnie fumbled for words, and clearly thought she had made her daughter angry by attempting to tie up loose ends at CCC with these two boys.

Phree grabbed Sunnie's shoulders and dipped nose to nose with her mother. "Who? Who did you say these boys are?"

Looking frightened, Sunnie said apologetically, "It doesn't matter. Like I said, I'll hand their case off to Dan."

"The names. Tell me their names."

"I…I don't know their real names. They're too scared to tell me, but their street names are Shark and Cardo."

Chapter 20
Phree

"Oh, my God." Phree bent at the waist, hands on knees, and gulped air like a runner who had just finished the last mile of a marathon. Sunnie was saying something, but Phree raised a hand off one of her knees in a palm-out 'stop' signal. Sunnie clamped her mouth shut, walked over to her daughter, and placed a steadying hand on her back. A few moments passed until Phree's breathing returned to its regular rate. She knew what the next step was. *I need proof.*

The digital scrapbook that Lettie had surprised them with a few years ago as a Christmas gift had individual pictures of all the families. Marge had hosted a summer picnic at her home that year, and it was a Kodak-moment extravaganza for the group. The bookcase in her sewing room displayed her photo albums, and Phree trailed her finger down the spines of all the digital books.

There it was! She snagged the top corner, and tugged it from the collection. Flipping between the pages she mumbled, "Where is it? Where is it?" Then, "Here," she said louder and spread the spine open. Sunnie was right behind her, watching over her shoulder, and Phree spun to face her confused mother. "Right here." She jabbed her finger at a picture. The smiling Mitchell family posed with arms around the person next to them. Ricky stood alongside Rosa, and they had tilted their heads toward each other, touching just above the ears. Tapping the photo, Phree said, "Is this him? Is this Cardo?"

Sunnie looked at the photo, and her face drained of color. She put one hand to her mouth and the other to her throat, as she inhaled a ragged gasp. Her eyes were the size of ping-pong balls as she whispered to her daughter, "Yes, that's him."

"What do you mean we can't just go off 'half-cocked' and call Rosa?" Phree's voice was high and louder than normal as she snatched her cell phone off the counter and glared at her mother. "It's June and her child—her baby—has been missing since last December. Of course we have to call Rosa. She needs to know right now."

Keeping her voice calm, Sunnie reached over and put her hand on Phree's lower back. "Give me five minutes to explain, and then if you still think that's the best plan of action, we'll contact her."

Sunnie held out her other hand for the phone. Phree hesitated. After surrendering the device, she grumbled something about not being five years old anymore, and that she didn't need her mother micromanaging her cell phone for her.

Sunnie ignored the complaining, and by maintaining gentle pressure to Phree's back, guided her toward the kitchen. They sat across from each other at the table, with the photo album resting sideways between them. It was open to the page showing the Mitchell family.

"I have dealt with runaways for decades, Phree. If we force the issue and Ricky isn't ready or willing to go back to his family, he'll be gone again by next week. And we have to think what that would that do to Rosa." She didn't wait for Phree to answer. This was not a dialogue—this was Sunnie capsulizing years of experience into a five-minute plea for understanding. "We both know it would destroy her. She's fragile, Phree. We have to be careful how we handle this for both her and Ricky's sake."

"But how...?"

This time Sunnie held up her hand. "Let me talk to Cardo...um Ricky. Let me find out where his mind is. He trusts me, and I think I can reach him. If I break that trust by telling his family where he is, he'll simply walk away and go deep underground. We risk losing all contact with him."

"What if it doesn't work? Is this even legal?"

"If it doesn't work, then he isn't ready to come back home. Is it legal?...not exactly, but our goal is to reunite the family so it sticks. If Ricky bolts after I talk with him, I'll have the police on his ass before he reaches the next block. That's when it will most likely get ugly, and the results will be iffy at best. But we will have at least attempted to intercede with the best intentions for both parties."

Phree exhaled a deep breath. "I don't know. It seems like a big gamble either way."

"It is, honey. We have to realize that the results are out of our hands. We can only proceed cautiously, and hope and pray for the best outcome. Now, can you give me any background as to why Ricky ran away in the first place? Were there problems at home? Were his parents cruel to him in any way?"

"He wasn't *ever* abused by Rosa or Terry." Phree stopped for a beat, "I guess it's true that you never really know what goes on behind closed doors, but I'd be shocked to find his parents mistreated him. As best as I can tell he was loved and adored… actually quite a momma's boy until about this time last summer. He connected with a group of bad kids, and it all went downhill after that."

"Can you think of anything that caused him to hang around with those kids, or maybe could have triggered such a drastic change in his behavior?"

"No. There's nothing. We've all discussed it over and over, and no one can figure out what happened to him. We just chalked it up to going through puberty."

Sunnie nodded her head, but inwardly thought that something must have prompted him to act out. "I'm going to head to City Care and have a little chat with Mr. Ricardo Mitchell." She tapped the photo of Ricky with her finger. "Will you be all right while I'm gone?"

"Yeah. I've got a ton of work at the retreat. I'm meeting with Claire, the kitchen designer, and we're going to go over some layouts for the kitchen in the retreat and the one in the Crow's Nest." Phree looked at her mother. "I think I really like that name. Thanks for the suggestion."

Sunnie saw warmth in her daughter's eyes along with something else—could it be admiration?

"I'll also give Claire a heads up that you'll be taking one of the suites. I'll have her work on some drawings for upgrading the kitchenette to be more practical for the needs of the new Assistant GM." Phree approached her mother with her arms out. "Hug? I think I need one."

Sunnie embraced her distraught daughter and gave her a tight squeeze. "It's going to work out for the Mitchells, sweetie. We've made the right decision."

"I'm afraid for Rosa either way, but I'm glad you're here and know how to handle this." Breaking the hug, Phree walked to the sink for the dishcloth, where she ran it under water and then squeezed it out. "I have to tell you that I'm really impressed with all that you're doing. It's kind of gotten overshadowed by all the Ricky stuff today, but I'm excited that we're going to be working together and living close to each other." Swabbing down the kitchen table she said, "I really do love you, you know."

Sunnie had waited her adult life for Phreedom to say those words. "And I love you more than anything, my baby girl. Now I'm going into the city to see if we can bring Ricky Mitchell home."

Chapter 21
Ricky

At almost twenty years old, Shark reminded Ricky of his older brother Alex. The two runaways had met at a homeless shelter on a frigid January night, and they had been watching out for each other ever since.

Ricky had kept an eye on the crazy pace of the falling snow. From several floors up and through oversized panels of glass, he watched as large, heavy flakes glided earthbound. Several times while looking down at street level, he observed a frigid wind as it spun the accumulated snow into drifts. Not only was the Harold Washington Library warm and quiet, but at this moment Ricky wished it was open all night. He had managed to stay out of the cold for most of January by coming here almost every day. But the bad news was that the temperature was due to drop into single digits sometime later tonight.

The library was huge, ten floors in all, and by staying somewhat clean, looking studious, and moving to different sections every few hours, he was able to maintain anonymity. As far as he could tell, no one suspected the polite, bookish boy to be a homeless, underage runaway.

Around 8:30 p.m. Ricky started his usual departure routine by respectfully returning any books or materials to their proper places. His backpack bulged from a small but warm blanket he had purchased at a thrift shop, along with an extra pair of jeans, a heavy sweater, and several pairs of socks. He was happy that he had been wearing a warm winter jacket, scarf, and gloves on the night he had bolted from Marge's

Christmas party with the Bunco jackpot money and several stolen electronic devices. As soon as he could, he sold the electronics for a shockingly small amount of cash to a heavily tattooed dude named Joker. Food was his biggest expense, and with a little over half of the money left, he hoped he could make it until spring.

His thoughts today, as on most days, had been consumed with struggling to figure out where he would spend the night. There was an abandoned building about ten blocks south where he had stayed with other homeless people for the past few weeks. Not only was it far away in this cold and snowy weather *and* at this time of night, but in Ricky's opinion there were also way too many druggies and drunken brawls on the premises for his liking.

Using a free computer with Wi-Fi at the library, he had researched shelters. In the past, he had stayed away from organized shelters, fearing he might get turned in to the police by some well-meaning volunteer because of his age. But today the weather had changed his mind. He was willing to risk what might happen for a warm bed, a nice shower, and a full belly. For a few dollars, he could take the CTA Red Line train and be at the Windy City Youth Center in twenty minutes.

The train jostled back and forth as it traveled north between stations. It would take seven or eight stops. Ricky couldn't remember exactly how many, but he would watch for the Belmont Avenue station. He noticed that several other passengers also stood as the train approached the station where he would disembark. Waiting in line to exit, the guy behind him had a backpack and a sports-type duffel bag. He said, "Dude, you going to Windy City?"

Ricky nodded slowly, cautious as always, and finally said, "Yeah. You?"

"Yeah, man." Another pause as the train jolted to a stop. "Ever been there before?"

"Nah. Have you?"

"A couple times when the weather's shitty like this." The doors whooshed open and the riders began to depart. The two homeless boys wordlessly fell into step and headed toward the shelter together. Ever since that night, Ricky felt a close bond to his street brother. As long as Shark was around, Ricky felt safe.

Keeping the main area of City Care clean was Cardo's duty in exchange for a clean bed and some food. As he swept the space and prepared to take out the trash, he watched Shark helping Dan with an intake. A young mother feared her baby was ill but didn't know what to do for him. Shark was holding the weeping, snuffling baby and gently bouncing him as the mother cried while answering Dan's questions. The mother had one black eye and bruises on her face and arms. Cardo figured that drugs were probably involved somehow. As far as he was concerned, Shark was becoming way too comfortable at City Care Chicago, and that made Cardo very anxious. While it was true that they had both enjoyed a roof over their head and three meals a day, Cardo (the only name Ricky had divulged at this point to anyone) still feared that something could go wrong, and that the police might be notified. Then he'd be forced to run again in order to keep his family, especially his mother, safe.

He had just gotten one of the full trash bag tops tied in a knot and billowed the new one to fit in the can when Sunnie walked into the area. Ricky thought she was spending time at a relative's house, but he was happy to see her. He liked Sunnie. She was kind to him, and as best he could tell, she had always been honest. She said she wouldn't turn him in to the authorities, and she hadn't. He had seen her doing some hand quilting in the evenings when she was around, and it reminded him of his mom. But Ricky wouldn't allow himself to think about his family; it was too painful.

Sunnie came toward him with her hand cupped to her mouth and in a low voice said, "Come on, let's take a break until that kid stops screaming. Don't tell anyone, but I stopped by Angelica's Bakery and picked up one of their famous Caramel Cakes. Have you ever had a slice?"

Ricky held up the trash bag. "I should probably…"

"Don't worry about it." She pointed to a corner with her chin. "Put it over there. You can take care of it when we're done."

Something felt a little off, but Ricky did as he was told and went to Sunnie's office. She had started to slice the cake, and the aroma nearly knocked him over. "I thought you were away at a relative's or something."

"I was." She looked up and smiled at him. Long, beaded earrings outlined her face like a fancy picture frame. "Close the door. I don't want anyone to see this cake until I can hide half of it. As soon as anyone knows it's here, word will spread faster than yawns at church."

Yes, Ricky liked this woman, and he thought that his mom would like her, too. They sat in silence as each took a forkful of cake. He watched as Sunnie closed her eyes and purred out a long, throaty "mmm." She looked at him and said, "My favorite. What do you think?"

Finishing another bite, he said, "This is great."

"Cardo, you know I'm resigning from CCC soon. I'm going to miss this place and all the wonderful people we are fortunate to meet here. …And that includes you." She swiveled her desk chair and took two bottles of water from a minifridge. "I'm not exactly sure how to say this, but I want you to promise that you will listen to everything I'm about to tell you before you make any decisions. Can you promise me that?"

He nodded his head, but the moist cake became difficult to swallow in his suddenly dry mouth. *I knew something was up. Where is she going with this?* His eyes darted around the room, bouncing from Sunnie, to a tall bookcase filled with haphazardly stacked and tilting books, to an empty sofa, and finally toward the door. The frightened boy worried there might be danger on the other side.

"Nobody's out there. I guarantee that I haven't, nor will I, call the police. You're safe here. You always have been, and you can trust me on that."

Sunnie had been straight with him the whole time he had stayed here. He decided he owed it to her to agree. Nodding, he whispered, "Okay."

"I discovered something interesting this morning and wanted to get your thoughts."

He could tell she was making a point by using direct eye contact, and he watched her face closely for any sign of deceit.

"As you said, I've been spending time with some relatives, and will be moving near my daughter and granddaughter after I tie up some loose ends and leave here."

She was unhurried and speaking deliberately, and this made Ricky even more anxious. Short, rapid breaths and intense fear made his nostrils flair. There was a pause as Sunnie took the last bite of cake, set the plate down, and looked at him for a long moment.

"My daughter…" She didn't finish the sentence but paused again. "My daughter lives in Whitney."

His head jerked to the door and then back at Sunnie.

"In fact, I believe you even know her. Phree Clarke."

"Oh, no." Ricky moaned. He stood and said more forcefully, "This is bullshit."

Sunnie stayed calm as he paced toward the door. With one hand on the doorknob and the other raking through his hair he said, "Seriously?"

"Sit down, Ricky. We have an agreement with each other, and I intend to honor my half as long as you honor yours."

She had used his real name! He sat, hung his head, and then tented his hands over his nose and mouth. As he lifted his eyes to hers, he dragged his hands down his face, stretching his cheeks and emitting a muffled, "Crap."

"I take it this is not good news."

"Have you seen my mom? Does she know I'm here? Is she okay?"

"Yes, I've met her several times. She's a very nice woman...but..."

"But what? No one's hurt her have they?"

Sunnie's brows curled, and Ricky detected confusion on her face. "That's a rather odd question. Why would you ask if someone has hurt her?"

"I...I don't know. Just tell me if she's okay."

"Aside from being worried out of her mind and not knowing if you're even alive—yeah, she's in good health."

He closed his eyes and slumped in his chair and thought *Thank God.* "So, does she know? Did you tell her?"

"The only one who knows is Phree, and she has promised me she won't go to your family until I've had a chance to talk with you."

"There's nothing to talk about. I can't go back." Big tough Ricardo Mitchell could feel tears in control of his eyes.

"What do you mean you *can't* go back? Have you been hurt? Is someone threatening you?"

He stood and spun toward the door, but did not move. Both hands were fisted above his ears and brown tufts of his long hair sprung from between his curled fingers. He could not stop his tears. He could not. So he doubled over and spat out a moan that was more like a loud, angry growl. Ricky hadn't heard her move, but Sunnie's arms were around him. She murmured into his ear like his mom used to do, and it made his knees weak with the joy of feeling loved again. Sobbing incoherent groans, first loud and finally softer, he allowed himself to hold Sunnie and hug back. She kept an arm firmly around him, as she guided him to the sofa that was used when families were in her office.

She didn't rush him. When his tears slowed enough, he wiped his nose on his sleeve and coughed. "I'm sorry…I'm…"

"That's okay, sweetie." She reached for a box of tissue and set it on the sofa. "A little snot hasn't hurt me yet."

Ricky found himself chuckling at her comment, which further caused his nose to run, and him to apologize again.

Sunnie held one of his hands, and used her other hand to brush sweaty hair from Ricky's face. "You okay?" She tilted his head so he would be forced to look directly at her, but his eyes remained downcast. "Look at me, Ricky. That's better. It's just you and me in here. No one else. Tell me what happened. What's going on. I think someone has scared you. Maybe even hurt you."

"I can't."

"You'll feel better if you aren't alone in this. Let me carry some of the burden for you."

"I…I want to, but I'm so afraid."

Chapter 22
Sunnie

She let him take his time. Ricky was struggling and was close to sharing something that had been so terrifying that the only option he felt he had was to run away. The sweet scent of Angeline's Caramel Cake filled the room, betraying the seriousness of the impending conversation. Sunnie placed an arm across Ricky's back, and he leaned in to her, resting his head on her shoulder like a little boy gaining strength from his mother. She stroked his knotted tangle of long hair, and his sobs quieted in both pace and depth.

From experience Sunnie knew that this was the point he would either talk or bolt. He could easily stand up and tell her he was feeling better and thank-you very-much. Stepping in before his thought process could formulate that option, she said, "If it helps at all, I'm a good listener. Nothing will leave this room without your permission. I respect that *you* know what's best for *you*."

Without lifting his head from the protection on her shoulder, he said, "It's…it's not something…I mean…I've never told anyone. If anyone found out they'd hate me."

"Is that why you haven't told your parents? Because you think they'd hate you?"

"I *know* they'd hate me. *I* hate me….but there's other reasons, too."

As Sunnie was beginning to piece together a scenario in her head, one that enraged her, she kept calm, and said, "Why don't you start at the beginning, honey."

Moments passed and she felt him heave a breath, deep into his lungs. As soon as he said, "There was this older guy…" Sunnie's blood ran cold.

It was only two o'clock in the afternoon, but after sharing the truth of his last nightmarish year, Ricky Mitchell was exhausted. Sunnie walked him to the room he shared with Shark and told him she'd wake him for dinner. Fully clothed, he wilted onto his bed under the weight of his recent admission. "I'll make a few calls while you rest." She perched herself on the corner of his bed and held one of his limp hands. "What happened to you is a crime, Ricky, a horrible crime. You are not at fault, my dear. *You* are the victim." He turned his head toward the wall. "I'm going to be the first in a long line of people that will reassure you that you are not to blame."

"But I could have…"

"Remember, honey, you were barely fourteen years old when this happened. Now, turn off your mind and get some sleep. You'll want to be fresh for tomorrow."

"I still think my mom is going to hate me."

"If there is one thing that I know for sure on God's green earth it's that your mother will *not* hate you because of this."

His eyelids were heavy and he blinked them several times until they finally remained closed. "I hope you're right because I really want to go home. I miss everyone so much."

"And I know, because I've seen it, just how much your family misses you too, Ricky."

She stayed with him, holding his hand, until his breathing became soft with the rhythm of a blessedly peaceful sleep.

Chapter 23
Phree

Kitchen, bath, and interior design goddess, Claire Givens, was Asian in looks, American by birth, and filled with inspired ideas. Bending over a set of floor plans and pointing to areas in the out-of-date kitchen of the MQR, she said, "We'll completely gut this room and knock that wall of the pantry down over there. That will give us more room to reconfigure the pantry/storeroom, and at the same time save space in the main part of the kitchen. See how much bigger this will be?"

Phree was grateful for the distraction of working with the designer. Until Claire had shown up, she had paced through the retreat in a daze, wondering what in the heck was going on with her mother and Ricky. At least now she was concentrating on the details of energy efficient appliances along with a greener approach to food preparation, storage, and waste management. "I love the idea of our own year-round greenhouse for fresh veggies," she told Claire. "I know the guests will appreciate the difference in taste."

"I suggest we install a large composter to help fertilize those yummy veggies as well as make use of any discarded organic materials by recycling them. We can coordinate a spot with the landscape architect. I'd like to keep it close enough to the backdoor so the kitchen staff will use it on a regular basis."

"For your needs to feed three meals a day plus snacks to as many as 50 guests and staff, I highly recommend this restaurant-style range and cooktop." Claire passed her client a color spec sheet of the sexiest stove that Phree had ever seen. "This is a multirange commercial unit that has a combination of gas burners for numerous tasks." Claire continued with handouts of various major and small appliances, touting the usefulness and necessity of each one.

After discussing and agreeing on every possible aspect for a state-of-the-art professional kitchen, Claire said, "Let's talk dining room."

"I thought we'd repurpose those beautiful, long tables and benches that are in there."

"I'm not sure that's your best option." Explaining that it can be anywhere from uncomfortable to impossible for some women to throw a leg over a long bench while balancing on another foot, she added, "If you're dead set on using these tables, I would recommend, at the very least, to use individual chairs."

"I hadn't thought of any of that, but you're right. Some of our quilters are sure to be elderly while others could be handicapped in some way. Maneuvering onto a long bench could be difficult. What thoughts do you have for alternative seating?"

"I'd like to see a beautiful restaurant-style dining room in here. I think it would go more with the image you plan to portray of a world-class retreat. I suggest perhaps all round tables of eight or ten, or a combination of round and square with a few booths along that wall. We can further class it up with any of these wonderful light fixtures." Holding out a brochure, Claire said, "I especially like this one. A series of these fixtures hanging overhead will add warmth to the room and at the same time greatly improve the '50s era lighting that's currently in there."

"I think you're right about the tables. I'd be better off not using these beauties for the dining room, but do you have any ideas what I can I do with them? I'd like to use them somewhere at the retreat."

"Maybe one or two could somehow be incorporated in the sewing area—a place for cutting boards or laying out projects. Maybe one of them could be a conference table in the administrative office, or even put one in the four-season sunroom you have planned. The benches are another story, but perhaps one or two on the wraparound porch could be nice. I'd like to see them bolted down because they can become unstable at times."

"Those are all great suggestions, Claire. I must say you seem to understand a lot about quilting and the needs of quilters."

Tapping a stack of papers on the tabletop to straighten them, she said, "My mom and aunties were all avid quilters. Many times our small apartment was turned into a weekend retreat where the four sisters would share their lives as they made *ibul* for their loved ones. *Ibul* is Korean for quilts."

"I'm ready to make an executive decision here." Phree straightened her posture and said, "We'll go with both round and square tables in the dining room, and I also like the idea of some booths along that wall." In her mind Phree could see the dining room filled with quilters eating meals at individual tables that were topped with crisp linens at dinnertime, and gleaming wooden tabletops during breakfast and lunch. Centered on each table would be eclectic vases with fresh cut flowers. Flapping the brochure back and forth, she said, "These light fixtures are perfect. Let's use them in here, too."

"I think those choices will make an inviting and enjoyable dining experience for your guests," Claire told her. "I assume we agree on keeping these lovely wood floors?"

"I absolutely agree on the floors. I also like that we will be able to utilize the dining room in a casual setting, but we'll still have the option to make it more elegant for the quilters' final dinner of the week."

"I'll pull together some ideas for window treatments in here for the next time we get together. Now..." Claire picked up her laptop and a handful of manila folders. "Shall we take a look at the kitchenettes in the suites? We can do a general upgrade for three of them and a kick-ass kitchen for your mom." As the women climbed the stairs she said, "While we're up here, I'll show you my ideas for improving the bathrooms."

It wasn't until after Claire had left with a promise to be back in three days, that Phree began to wonder how things were going with Sunnie and Ricky Mitchell. Not for the first time that day she wished her mom could have been at the retreat, helping her as a sounding board for Claire's ideas. She wandered back to the suite that her mother was designated to occupy and still couldn't believe that Sunnie and she were going to be working and living this close together. Phree had asked Claire to work on some ideas that would make this suite particularly nice and cozy. Looking out the picture window, Sunnie would have a bird's-eye view of the Crow's Nest from here, and vice versa.

Phree's cell phone rang and she slipped it from her pocket. Sunnie's picture had popped up on the screen, and Phree slid her finger across the glass to answer.

"We have good news. He's ready. I'd like you to help with Rosa and Terry."

"Anything you need."

It seemed that her mother, Sunnie Eaton, had just pulled off the impossible by convincing Ricky Mitchell to come back home. Phree felt her chest puff with pride for the scrawny little woman who had annoyed her for a good portion of her life. A bolt of clarity hit as she wondered how many times this was what Sunnie had been doing for some other desperate family when she, Phreedom Aquarius, had so selfishly been pouting.

Sunnie explained that being this close to a reunion, she didn't want Ricky to get cold feet. She thought it best if she stayed at City Care tonight in case Ricky needed to talk more. After learning what had happened, she was confident that Ricky's leaving home was not due to abusive or negligent parents. The best thing for Ricky Mitchell was to be reunited with his family.

"Tomorrow morning can you ask Rosa if she and Terry can come down to my office at City Care? Don't call them tonight. They'll only go crazy with worry, and Ricky is too exhausted to do this right now. Explain that I have something I want to tell them. That I have news about Ricky, but wouldn't say what it is."

"Why don't you bring Ricky back here—to his home? Wouldn't that make more sense?"

"It's best if they have neutral ground for this meeting. Home is too familiar to all of them. Mom starts fussing with getting food into him or getting him into clean clothes. Sometimes Dad disappears and takes off to work because he can't deal with the emotions, or he can even become aggressive—insisting on answers or actions. And the last thing we want is the runaway to feel trapped before reconciliation even starts."

"I had no idea..."

"Don't feel bad, honey. There wouldn't be a reason for you to be aware of any of this."

"Then what happens?"

"Ricky is still convinced his parents will hate him."

"Why would..."

Sunnie interrupted. "It's a long story, and one that I'm not at liberty to tell at this point. But he has essentially been hurt and brainwashed, for lack of a better word, by an evil person."

"Oh my God," Phree whispered. "That poor kid."

"He wants me to tell his parents what happened last summer without him in the room. And then I'll leave Mom and Dad in my office while I tell Ricky that, indeed, they still love him and want him to come home. We have to remember that he just turned fifteen a few days ago, and he was handling this the best way his young mind could."

"I'll text you after I give the Mitchells your message in the morning."

Chapter 24
Rosa

The people and scenery of Chicago's South Side on busy Stony Island Avenue was a blur to Rosa as she once again asked her husband why he thought Sunnie wanted to see them. Terry drove a little too fast, but then again *everyone* on Stony seemed to be driving faster than the speed limit. A driver cut them off, and zigzagged between the three lanes in an attempt to get ahead of others.

"Let's not get our hopes up, Rosa. I think that most likely someone from the street probably mentioned something about Ricky, and Sunnie put two and two together. I'll bet that's exactly what happened."

"But why would she have us drive down here? Couldn't she tell us about it the next time she was in Whitney? She's at the retreat almost every day."

"Maybe the eyewitness wants to talk to us for some reason. I don't know, babe, but we're almost there, and we'll find out soon."

Parking was a precious commodity in the city, and the Mitchells felt fortunate to find a spot only two blocks away from Sunnie's office. One beat shy of running, the couple held hands as they fast-walked toward City Care Chicago. It was a warm end-of-June day in the suburbs, but a breeze off Lake Michigan funneled through the city streets and chilled Rosa. Her hair whipped off to the side and around her face, while ragged breaths puffed through her lungs. She and Terry were both slightly winded by the time they reached City Care Chicago's complex.

She had never had a reason to be here before, and the group of buildings was larger than she had imagined. Entering a courtyard, she felt momentarily confused where they should enter, and she stopped walking. Terry gave a gentle nudge and guided her toward one of several doors.

"We're almost there," he said. "Whatever Sunnie knows, we'll deal with it together."

A twenty-something woman, who reminded Rosa of a younger version of Sunnie, was vacuuming a carpeted seating area as they entered. Flipping the switch on the ancient Hoover to off, she smiled and said, "I'm sorry. I hope you haven't been waiting too long. Can I help you?"

"We're the Mitchells, and we're here to see Sunnie Eaton," Terry said. "She's expecting us."

"Yes, she told me you were coming. Follow me, please."

Rosa's sixth sense was on high alert, and she picked up on a slight double take that the receptionist gave them. *She knows something.* Sunnie greeted them in her office with a comfortable smile that did *not* convey bad news, and Rosa let out a breath she had been holding for what seemed like the hour it took them to get here.

"Have a seat." She pointed to two chairs in front of a large desk. "I'm just going to close this door. Megan is a wonderful volunteer, but unfortunately she's obsessive about vacuuming. The noise can get rather annoying."

Whether that was true or not, Rosa was happy for the privacy.

"I'm sure you're wondering why I wanted to see you." Both Mitchells nodded. Rosa could not speak. "I'll get right to the point. I have some information about your son Ricky."

Rosa felt weak. She felt hot and cold all at once. Her chest burned with a searing jolt of adrenaline, and she started shaking. Sunnie swiveled in her desk chair and reached into the minifridge for two bottles of water. She handed one to each of her guests without an explanation, but said, "Are you okay, Rosa?"

"Tell me."

"He's fine."

"You've seen him?"

"Yes, quite a bit. I've seen him and he's safe."

"Why didn't you tell me before? Where is he?"

"I've only known him by his street name, Cardo, for several weeks now. After his birthday party the other night at The Depot, I discovered his identity. Ricky and I spent much of yesterday discussing what happened to him. He wants to come home, Rosa. He misses his family."

Sobs and laughter mingled, while Rosa attempted to form words. Sunnie slid a box of tissue closer to the tearful couple. Through tears of his own, Terry asked, "Where is he? We want to see him."

"Ricky has trusted me with what happened, and he has some information he wants me to share before you are reunited."

Rosa felt confused and impatient all at the same time. "Tell us, so we can see him."

"Some of this might be hard to hear. He's convinced…no, he has been coerced into thinking that you won't love him if you know the details."

"We will *never* not love him. He's my child. How could he think that?" Fear and anger wrestled with each other in Rosa's mind.

"Let's hear what Sunnie has to tell us, babe. The sooner she does, the sooner we'll see Ricky." Terry gave her hand a gentle squeeze.

"Apparently, Ricky had a friend in grade school named David Hoffman. Did you know him?"

Terry answered. "Yeah, they were pretty tight buddies until about a year ago. He was a good kid, nice family. A group of boys used to hang out at each other's homes, playing video games and watching movies. They were at the Hoffman home the most, I'd say." Rosa nodded in agreement. "Sometime last summer, right around the time Ricky started acting up, they stopped seeing each other. I asked him several times why he wasn't friends with David anymore, and all Ricky would tell me was that David was 'lame' or a 'tool'. What does he have to do with all this?"

"Directly, nothing. But indirectly…this is where it gets difficult." Rosa noticed Sunnie take a deep breath and stare over their shoulders for a moment. "When the group of boys were at David's they often went across the street to a neighbor's house. Ricky only knew this man's name as Jimmy."

"Man?" Terry said.

Sunnie nodded. "At some point, your son had gone to David's house to hang out, and no one was home. He thought his buddies were probably all over at Jimmy's. There had been talk of some kind of video game tournament that Jimmy was talking about hosting. Once inside, Ricky discovered the others were not there." Sunnie paused for a moment, wishing she didn't have to tell these parents what had happened to their little boy. "…and he was alone with Jimmy."

"NO!" Rosa moaned, tears streaming. "No! No!"

"I'm sorry, Rosa. I'm so very sorry."

Terry slammed his fist on the desk and stood. Rosa watched as her tender husband's face crumpled in sadness. He leaned forward, rested both palms on the desk, and spat out to Sunnie, "Who is this bastard. What's his name?"

Rosa tugged on Terry's sleeve. "Sit down, luv. Sit down. Let's hear the rest."

"I know there was abuse. I'm not sure of the details. Ricky told me that Jimmy threatened to harm his family, specifically Rosa, if he didn't cooperate. Before Ricky left that day, Jimmy made your son promise he'd come back or he would…" Sunnie paused and pulled two tissues from the box for herself. "He would stab Rosa with a butcher knife until he killed her."

A raggedy gasp caught in Rosa's throat as all the implications of this horrible story crashed through her brain. After a full year of questioning what had happened to her sweet boy, she was sickened to hear the truth. Closing her eyes, she rested her elbows on the desk, and placed her head in her hands. Terry was standing again and this time walked over to the wall and punched it, while spitting out, "Son of a bitch," between tightly clenched teeth. "I'll kill the bastard."

"I'm sorry," Sunnie said. "I'm so sorry you have to hear this, but please sit down, Terry. We need to focus on Ricky first, and plan for the best way to help him. We'll nail that asshole as soon as your son is safely back home."

"Come on Terry. Sit down. Sunnie's right, we've got to stay calm."

Starting with the day that Cardo had brought Shark to City Care Chicago for an intestinal problem, Sunnie told the stunned Mitchells everything she knew about their son. Her steady voice and constant praise for Ricky soothed Rosa. "I could tell he was a good kid from the first time I met him. He has a good heart. He's just been scared out of his mind. After he went to juvie and Jimmy hadn't harmed his mom, he thought that if he ran away you'd be safe. It was the only way he knew to protect you."

Anguish left Rosa numb. It burned in her chest and throbbed in her head. She only wanted to feel her arms around her boy again. To hold him, to soothe his pain, to let him know he was still loved. Terry was grieving, and it came across in a typical male way—through aggression.

Rosa asked, "What do we do? How can we help him?"

"I want you both to understand that this will be a long-term healing process for the whole family. It's sad to say, but I've worked with countless runaways and their families over the years. The good news is that by following some specific guidelines with a lot of hard work and love, eventually you'll have success. The number one most important thing to do for all four family members is counseling. Ricky will be dealing with multiple issues, and he's going to need your support. The two of you will also need help to know how to guide him back to a hopeful life again *and* to learn how to deal with your own grief over what happened. And Alex will most likely have some problems and concerns as well."

Rosa was crying—not sobbing, not gushing, but rather a steady constant sadness was seeping out and manifesting itself through her tears. Sunnie softened her voice. "I know how much you both love your children, and I can tell you'd do anything for them. I'm confident you're up for this challenge. It's time to be strong, because we also have to go after that bastard, Jimmy. We can't let him harm another child. I suggest you inform Brian of what happened as soon as possible. Let him handle that end of things. You two concentrate on Ricky." Sunnie looked from Rosa to Terry, and then back at Rosa. "What do you think? Are we ready?"

Rosa looked at her husband. "Yes, let's bring our baby home."

Chapter 25
Sunnie

It had gone well with the Mitchells, about as well as could be expected and about exactly as Sunnie had thought it would. Now for the reunion. She walked around her desk, toward the door as she said, "I'll get Ricky. Just a few more minutes, and you'll be together again."

Ricky had not wanted to be in the room when Sunnie talked with his parents, and had agreed he would wait in the reception area until she came out of her office to retrieve him. Expecting to see Ricky Mitchell when she turned left at the end of the hall, Sunnie was surprised to see only Megan. She was bent over the upturned vacuum cleaner pulling on a long piece of yarn that had twirled up in one of the wheels. "Is Ricky here?"

She assumed she'd hear something like 'he went to the bathroom.' Instead Megan said, "He left about ten minutes ago."

"Left?"

She pointed toward the door with a nod of her head. "Yeah. He just got up and walked out. Didn't say anything."

Sunnie's heart almost bumped through her rib cage. *Oh my God. What the hell am I going to tell Rosa?*

Chapter 26
Phree

What was taking so long? Her mother was supposed to call as soon everything was over and the Mitchells were all heading back home. She had phoned Rosa at 8:30 that morning telling her Sunnie wanted to talk to them, and now it was nearly one o'clock in the afternoon. Had they hit a snag? Phree couldn't come up with a single thing that made sense for such a long delay. She had envisioned Rosa swooping in, grabbing Ricky, and not letting go until he was 30 years old, and that should have taken only fifteen minutes once they got there.

Meanwhile, Phree was knee-deep in appointments today. The representative for the solar panel company had run half an hour into the tuck-pointers' time. She was excited that it was estimated solar energy would provide half the electricity for the retreat. It was a good thing that she had blocked off forty-five minutes for lunch. By the time the tuck-pointers checked out the bricks on both the retreat and the Crow's Nest, she had ten minutes to gulp down a very dry turkey sandwich. She was biting into an apple when Claire showed up with suggestions for paint colors, an array of tiles, bathroom faucets, and numerous samples of light fixtures.

The noise of construction at the MQR never stopped between the hours of 7:00 a.m. and somewhere around six in the evening. Drills, hammers, scraping, sanding, and whirring circular saws became a daily symphony as the team of workers coaxed the old convent into a quilters dream. Claire shouted over the sounds, "This is all second floor stuff today. Let's go upstairs where it might be a little quieter." Phree helped by hoisting one of several boxes that Claire had schlepped inside and then carried it for her.

They passed the area where space for the elevator was being created and headed toward the main staircase. As they reached the upper level, the loud sounds from downstairs diminished, but were replaced with soft rasping swooshes made by three women from Paint the Town Pink, an all-female paint contractor. They were in the process of repairing all the cracks in the old-fashioned plaster walls. The owner of the company, sporting a dust mask and white painter's coveralls, waved at Phree as she passed by.

"Let's head to Sunnie's suite where we can spread out the proposals. Earlier today I brought up a card table and a few chairs for the meeting."

"That'll be helpful. I have some sketches for making your mother's apartment feel more homey and inviting. While these are nice-sized suites, they're a little bare-bones and cold." The two women entered Sunnie's future home and closed the door to further muffle the sounds. "Do you think your mother would like to be involved in the decision-making process?"

"My mom would *not* want any fuss. She would think there was nothing wrong with the space as it is. She's very low-maintenance. I'd like to surprise her with something real nice, so have a ball in here. Be as creative as possible."

As Claire set a bundle of samples and printouts on the card table, she rested her computer bag on the floor, and said, "I could just hug you. You've been the most fun client I've ever had. I'd like to get started on your home out back in the next few days. But first, I have a ton of ideas for this suite that will make it uniquely Sunnie's. From what I've seen she's quite a character and also extremely creative. It must be awesome to have her for a mom."

"Oh, she's awesome, all right." Phree felt a touch of pride but a lot of shame over the unkind way she'd acted toward Sunnie for such a long time. "After all these years, I think I'm finally beginning to understand and appreciate her."

Chapter 27
Ricky

Scared. Scared and happy. His mom and dad were in the same building, under the same roof as him.

Sunnie was so sure they would still love him that he had started to believe her. Since yesterday all he could think of was going home and being happy again. He was tired of being afraid, tired of not knowing where he would sleep, tired of avoiding drunken crazies and drugged-out thieves trying to steal from him. He wanted to be able to get hugs from his parents and feel loved. He wanted to be the person he used to be—before Jimmy happened. Sunnie had assured him that Jimmy was a lying scumbag about killing his mom. She told him that Brian would handle him, and it would be safe for him to go home.

Looking at the price tag and doing some simple calculations, he said, "I'll take three of these." As the stems of the red roses were dripping water after being taken from the large vase in the walk-in fridge, he called to the salesperson, "Could you add one more, please? And could I have that one wrapped separately?"

He planned to also hand a rose to Sunnie as he left City Care Chicago with his mom and dad.

Chapter 28
Sunnie

Maybe he went outside to walk off his anxiety or to get some fresh air. Sunnie stepped through the door to the brightness of outside, and shaded her eyes with a hand, looking first left then right in the empty courtyard. "Damn." She headed toward the street.

Opening the gate that leads to Stony Island from the sheltering cocoon of City Care Chicago's courtyard, Sunnie wasn't sure what she thought she'd find. If Ricky wanted to disappear, he had a busy city street that ran north and south through the heart of Chicago's South Side to help him vanish. City Care was respected in this neighborhood, and Sunnie was fearless as she looked up and down the street among both residents and transients. *Where the hell could he be, and what the heck happened to scare him off?*

She was about to turn around and head back to her office, where Rosa and Terry Mitchell were waiting for a reunion that was apparently not going to happen. A half block away, on the opposite side of the street, she spotted Ricky leaving Bonita's Flowers with what looked like a white paper-wrapped bundle of flowers. He was headed back to CCC, and when he saw her, he waved and picked up his pace.

Her heart flooded—she could feel it happen—the tenderness for this boy engulfed her chest and for the second time that day she swept away tears. He approached her with a big, innocent smile on his face. Ricky appeared more at ease and happier than she had ever seen the boy Cardo. Sunnie slipped her arm around his shoulders and he around her waist as she matched his pace. Walking into City Care courtyard, she said, "You had me scared to death."

"I wanted to give my mom something, and I know how much she likes flowers." Ricky jostled the packages in his arms and held one out to her. "This is for you. To thank you."

She saw him blush, and a swelling knotted her throat. "Thank you, sweetie, that's very nice."

"You were..." he hesitated and looked off into the distance. The young boy's eyes held struggles of someone much older than fifteen. "I mean...you were nice. You made me believe in myself again."

While she wanted to sit somewhere quiet, reflect on the past several decades of helping others, and weep with joy, she guided Ricardo Mitchell, her last 'boy lost,' over the threshold of City Care Chicago and toward the loving arms of his parents.

For Sunnie, this had turned out to be one hell of a swan song.

Chapter 29
Rosa

The Mitchells paced the wooden floor of Sunnie's spacious office. *Where was he?* Their son was supposed to be right down the hall—surely it couldn't take this long for him to walk from Point A to Point B. "Something must be wrong," Rosa said. And then she asked her husband, "What do you think is going on?" And finally, "I'm so afraid that he might have changed his mind." Rosa sent up another silent prayer and ended it with the sign of the cross.

After each question, Terry attempted to calm his wife by explaining that Sunnie was most likely telling Ricky what they had discussed and reassuring him that he was loved and welcomed back home. "We need to be patient and trust Sunnie." The anxious parents eventually stopped pacing and talking. They simply held each other and attempted to buoy their flagging hopes, while their tears mingled together through Rosa's muffled sobs.

The door clicked.

Sunnie said, "Take as long as you'd like." She opened the door further, and there he was. Gasps, and then laughter, tears, and smiles completed the reunion—the runaway boy was back in the arms of his loving parents.

Watching the reunited family for a few more seconds, Sunnie mopped at her tears and left the Mitchells to begin the long process of healing.

Chapter 30
Rosa

Even though Ricky had been asleep upstairs for over an hour, Rosa found herself whispering. "You *both* have to promise me that you will *not* go over to this Jimmy person's house. Not now or ever." Alex had just heard the account of what had happened to his brother last summer, and his reaction was similar to his father's—he wanted to head straight to Jimmy's house and hurt the creep. "We have to stay focused on Ricky's well-being. We'll leave the rest to Brian. He's going to take care of Jimmy. I don't need either one of you spending your life in prison because you want to get even."

Alex was leaning against the counter and pushed himself to standing. "You don't understand, Mom. I want to see this asshole suffer."

"And you think I don't?" Rosa said. "And trust me, I *do* understand how your mind works. I have two male children and am married to a man. After all these years I know how the male mind works. There will be *no* pummeling first and worrying about the consequences later. Do you both understand?" She stood, narrowed her eyes, and pointed first at Terry and then at Alex. "If you cross me on this, I swear, prison will look like a cakewalk compared to what I'll do to you."

Rosa Maria Sanchez Mitchell was back in position as matriarch of their family unit, and, as head gatekeeper, she had just put everyone on lockdown.

"Congratulations." Brian smiled and thrust his palm out to shake each of the Mitchells' hands. "Nedra texted me last night and said Ricky was home." He motioned to two chairs in front of his massive desk. "Have a seat." Walking behind the desk he said, "What brings you here today?"

"I'm afraid it's not good news." Terry started to relay the story of their son's abuse. Brian scrawled notes on his legal pad, and when Terry became too choked up to continue, Rosa took over. Within only minutes, everything they knew about the attacks had been shared with their lawyer and friend. Brian had gone from smiles, to a worried brow, to conviction to catch the pedophile that had stolen a boy's innocence and caused him to live in fear for the past year.

"Let me see what I can find out about this guy, and I'll get back to you." Brian paused and Rosa knew he had more to say. "I am deeply sorry that this happened to your son. It explains his unusual behavior since last summer. As difficult as it is, I *strongly* advise that you *not* attempt to deal with this man on your own. Let me handle this with the help of the police."

"I don't want this to be public knowledge at this point," Rosa said. "Ricky's broken and scared, and I don't think he could handle everyone knowing what happened to him right now." She knew Brian would understand and trusted him to do what was necessary. "We're going to get Ricky into counseling in the next few days. I pray it will help him."

"As do I," the lawyer said. "Leave this ugliness to me. You two go home and rejoice that your child is back where he belongs."

Chapter 31
Phree

A real date. It was a rarity in Phree's life, and something she would try to keep from a too nosy mom and a daughter who would be horrified. Horrified as in, 'Aren't you too old for dating?' and then followed by 'Eew that's gross.' The less the supervisors-of-all-things-Phree knew, the better for Bill and her.

Telling the two 'wardens' that she was going to Nedra's for a quick carryout dinner and then work on the Mayflower quilt they were designing together, Phree was able to leave her house at 6:00 p. m. knowing that Sunnie would be staying with her daughter for the evening. Some might say she was being overprotective, but with The Bastard on the loose, it was better, as the saying went, to be safe than sorry.

A quick call to Nedra brought her into the ruse. "Yeah, I'll cover for you if necessary. No problem. And by the way, I actually do have some ideas for our much neglected Mayflower quilt. I took the two days off after the Fourth of July holiday, and I thought I might head over to the retreat to fill you in." After months of planning and renovating the retreat, Phree thought it sounded wonderful for a change to spend some time chatting about quilting with a friend.

With her ducks in a row, and dressed in a new top, khaki capris, and flip-flops, she headed toward Bill's home and a big-girl night out. She knew that if she pushed her attire to a more elaborate tier, she would surely trigger Sunnie's bullshit detector. Phree rationalized excuses to hide her plans for the evening, until she finally scolded herself. "For goodness sake, you're 38 years old—you don't have to report to anyone what you are doing or why."

Lieutenant Bill Hayden had been assigned to monitor Phree's house last fall when the story broke in the national news that she was the person who had discovered the Mayflower treasure. Isolated by several weeks of short-lived notoriety, Phree welcomed his 'check-in' knocks at her door. They found they had several things in common, not the least of which were ugly divorces. After the hype from the Mayflower announcement settled down, Bill was taken off surveillance, and a week later they went to dinner together. It was a slow-growing relationship, but Phree was fine with that. Her priority was maintaining a stable home life for her daughter, and that did *not* include dating until Emily was away at college. But with Sunnie in the picture, she decided a night out with a sexy cop could work into the time line.

A gentle rain had cleansed the air for the past few hours, and sunshine was beginning to break through the clouds. It smelled ozone fresh as Phree's car splashed through puddles that were quickly vanishing down the sewer drains. Feeling more than ready for a clandestine evening with a man, she pulled her car right on time down his driveway and parked in front of the detached garage. Bill lived in a duplex in a newly developed section of Whitney. She tugged on the visor and checked her teeth in the mirror, slipped yet another breath mint into her mouth, and reached for her purse.

Bill was standing at the grill wearing a manly Chicago Blackhawks barbeque apron over jeans and a polo shirt. He looked up from swabbing rain water off the outdoor furniture with an oversized towel, and walked toward Phree as she opened the car door. "I'm so glad you could make it tonight." He bent and kissed her cheek. "And, might I add, that you look lovely, Ms. Clarke."

"Why thank you, kind sir." Phree tucked her arm into his, and they headed for the patio. "And, might I add, that this is just what the doctor ordered. Thanks for suggesting a quiet evening at home."

"Shall we have drinks on the patio, or would you rather take your libations indoors?"

"Let's start on the patio unless the mosquitos get too bad."

Phree had enjoyed Bill's company from the first time they met. While she had seen him for years around Whitney in his official capacity as a police officer, they had never spoken until about a year ago. A concerned neighbor had called the police because she heard screams coming from Phree's home. Officer Hayden was dispatched to determine what was going on at the residence. Phree happened to be hosting an extremely rowdy Bunco club at her house, where Rosa had broken their standing record of most Buncos thrown in one game. Yes, there was much screaming that night, when she opened the door to Officer Hottie, as the Bunco girls called him.

What a pleasure it was to be with a considerate man, and not a self-serving, self-centered idiot like her ex-husband. She knew she needed to quit comparing Bill and Gary to each other, but it was too much fun *not* to take note of the extreme differences. "Can I help with anything?"

Phree asked, but secretly hoped he'd say no.

"Nah, I've got it. Sit there and relax."

Good answer. "What a beautiful evening. It always seems so fresh after a cleansing rain." Phree leaned her head back slightly and inhaled the sweetness of wet grass, humidity, and twilight.

"I thought I'd get the fire pit going a little later to keep us warm. It gets pretty chilly after the sun goes down."

While Phree wanted to say, "I've got a few other ideas to keep us warm," instead she said, "Great idea."

Handing a glass of wine to Phree and sitting next to her on the hardwood glider, he held his wineglass up for a toast. "To us."

"To us," she repeated and smiled, as they each took a sip.

"Tell me about the progress on your house. How's it going?"

Phree filled him in on what was happening at the Crow's Nest.

"Perfect name," he laughed. "I love it."

"Between Claire-the-designer and Nate-the-contractor it's going to be stunning when it's done. And that's before Bud-the-electrician and Jim-the-landscape architect have had any input." She described that viewing the Crow's Nest from the retreat, with the exception of siding, a new roof, and a few flower beds, it wouldn't look too much different than it did right now. Phree explained how she didn't want her guests at the MQR to feel as though she were showing off. "But from the side that faces the woods, it's going to be spectacular. They're practically gutting the whole inside, and there will be a large bank, and I mean a *very* large bank, of windows facing the trees. It will be stunning, but best of all I think it's going to be very peaceful."

"I'm happy for you. You deserve it."

She studied him for a beat, trying to tell if he was sucking up because of her money—though she didn't think this was the case with Bill. It certainly was something she never had to worry about before the Mayflower discovery. She saw kindness in his eyes—soft and sincere. "Thank you."

Phree questioned him about work at the station, and Bill, in turn, asked about progress on the retreat as well as updates about Sunnie and Emily. They both danced around the Ricky Mitchell topic, neither wanting to discuss the sad truth behind why a fourteen-year-old boy had run away from home. Phree knew there were probably specific points about the ongoing search for the offender that would be confidential police information, and she didn't want to come across as though she were prying.

The 'man of her dreams' started the gas grill as they continued talking, and then went inside to retrieve what he called his version of surf and turf. "I admit to grilling a mean steak, and my salmon's not bad either." Two glistening filet mignons sprinkled with spices rested next to foil wrapped packages of salmon. The meat sizzled as Bill lowered the slabs of beef onto the cooking grid with a pair of metal tongs. He left the salmon packets on the plate. "I'm guilty of being a bit of a foodie."

"I'm impressed," said Phree. "I don't know many men who like to cook...heck, I don't know many women who do either. How'd that happen?"

"I guess you could say survival. Long story short, Mom was a raging alcoholic, I was the oldest of three, Dad split when I was ten, and someone needed to step up to see that my sisters were fed. At first, I hated it. The word *gourmet* would never have been associated with my ten-year-old cooking skills. By the time I went to the police academy, I had started to experiment more. Once the food channel happened, I was completely sucked in." Palms up he said, "What can I say?"

"What happened to your sisters? Who fed them when you went away?"

"Blessedly, they didn't stay seven and five forever." He laughed and the lines around his eyes crinkled. "They both still hate to cook, but somehow they managed not to starve after I left home."

"And your mom?"

"Gone," he said without emotion. "She lost the booze battle without ever fighting it. Just couldn't control herself, I guess."

"I'm sorry," Phree said. "That must have been difficult." She thought of her years of angst over Sunnie not being the kind of mother she had wanted and felt a little ashamed and extremely shallow.

"Oh, it was plenty difficult. I try to remind myself that it made me strong, and that things could always be worse.

Besides, I doubt I would have picked up such a great hobby as cooking otherwise."

Phree wanted to say, "Are you for real? I'm pissing and moaning because I thought my mother paid more attention to other people than to me. Imagine my wallowing if I had to take care of two younger siblings at the age of ten." But instead she said, "That's a great attitude."

"Enough of the past." Bill stood. "It's time to flip the steaks and get the salmon on the grill. We have fresh asparagus along with my twist on a Caesar salad. I thought we'd eat dinner inside, and have dessert on the patio once the fire pit has warmed up the area. Is that okay with you?"

"That sounds incredible."

Phree was charmed.

Soft music played in the background. Dinner was spectacular. Conversation flowed nicely. The table setting was unembellished except for a solitary candle, but it had clean linens and a contemporary feeling—about what one would expect of a single man. And Officer Hottie was…well, hot.

As they rose to retire to the patio for dessert, Bill explained, "While I love to cook, I'm not much of a baker. I hope you don't mind something simple."

"Are you kidding? I'm not above opening a bag of chocolate chips and eating them before the cookie part has been added. In other words, don't worry, I'm not a dessert snob."

"Let me get…"

Their heads snapped to the front of his town house, where squealing tires sounded loud and close. "I'm going to pretend I didn't hear that," Bill said. "I'm officially off duty, and unless it's an emergency, somebody else can see if it's a 10-94."

"A 10-94? What's that?"

"Drag racing," he answered. "Anyway, could you grab the afghan on the sofa and bring it outside, while I get the fire pit going?"

Phree had nestled into the warm knitted throw (which was not *nearly* as warm as a handmade quilt, though she wouldn't be mentioning this detail to her host) when Bill carried a tray with dessert from the house. "Don't get too excited," he said, "but I thought this might be fun." He lifted a towel off a basket and showed Phree the contents.

"S'mores—perfect! I love them, and it's been forever since I've had one."

"Whew, I was afraid maybe this would be a little too low-key."

Tossing the afghan aside, Phree roasted the marshmallows over the fire pit on a long-handled, campfire-type fork. Bill assembled about a half dozen of the sweet treats on a plate before they decided that was probably enough. Phree had mentioned that she'd prefer not to drink any more wine after dinner; she'd be driving herself home and was aware of her limits. Her host had made two mugs of peppermint tea to go with dessert.

The couple snuggled close together under the knitted throw chatting softly, drinking tea, and eating s'mores. Phree could not think of a better date if her life depended on it.

Conversation slowed with the warmth of the fire and the mood turned serious when Bill put his arm around Phree and drew her closer. She nuzzled into his side and appreciated that s'mores were not the only thing she hadn't had in a long time. In unsaid agreement, they had taken their time getting to know each other before they did anything more serious. Phree knew that nothing major would happen tonight, but a little make-out session was not out of the question. When tires screeched on the road in front of Bill's house again, neither of them noticed.

Chapter 32
Rosa
June Board Meeting of the Mayflower Quilters Retreat

Rosa was *not* late for the second board members meeting at the Mayflower Quilters Retreat. As a matter of fact, when she drove her vehicle down the winding lane to the large building, which now sported a freshly painted friendship quilt block, her car was the first one in the parking lot. Two weeks had passed since Terry and she had brought Ricky home from City Care Chicago. Other than Sunnie stopping by every day to chat with her son and offer support and guidance to the whole family, Rosa had not seen any of her friends. She had conveyed through Sunnie that the family would like to have some privacy, and all of the women agreed to let the Mitchells reunite in peace.

Tonight, with Sunnie's help, she would cautiously inform the rest of the women what had happened to Ricky and how the family was handling the situation. Jimmy, the pedophile, had slipped through their fingers. Speculation was that when he found out Ricky had run away, he became spooked and took off. The other theory was that this probably wasn't his first incident, and he knew how to disappear—as in completely vanish. The police and Brian were doing everything they could, but the house Jimmy lived in had been rented to a family shortly after he vacated it. There would be no way that his fingerprints could be isolated among all the people that had come and gone over the past six months. Phree was forwarding money through Brian to pay for a private detective, but as of yet there were only dead ends to be reported.

The police had called in a sketch artist who came to the Mitchells home rather than forcing Ricky to go to the police station. He had worked with him for hours and together they created an image of the man who had caused an innocent boy so much pain. After all the warnings and threats Rosa had made to Terry and Alex to steer clear of the creep, she could have killed him herself when she saw the sketch for the first time.

When the drawing was finished, detectives had shown it to the other boys who had been hanging out at Jimmy's last summer. They all identified the drawing, but none of them knew where he was or anything helpful about him. "He just left in the middle of the night," said David Hoffman's father, who lived across the street from Jimmy. "We wondered what happened to him. What's this all about?"

The officer had been vague. "We need to find him to ask him some questions. That's all."

"He seemed like a nice guy. The kids all liked him and were sad when he left."

When the detective had told her about the conversation with Mr. Hoffman, Rosa wondered how a group of adults, her included, could have been so trusting and clueless. She would spend the rest of her life blaming herself for not realizing what was going on that summer in a small bungalow across the street from David Hoffman's home.

She jolted when Phree's car pulled alongside hers. "Sorry I'm late. I got a little tied up with a phone call from Claire, the interior designer."

"No worries. I'm actually early for once in my life. I was sitting here thinking how peaceful this property is." It was a bit of a lie, but the quilters compound truly was peaceful. "By the way, the friendship block on the building looks amazing. This is the first time I've seen it." Rosa popped the trunk of her car as Sunnie exited Phree's van on the passenger's side.

"Long time no see," Sunnie said. They had, in fact, spent several hours together last night finishing up a surprise project for Phree, after Sunnie had visited with Ricky. "Can I give you a hand?"

"No, but thanks. I've got it." Rosa took a large tote bag from the rear of her car and hitched it on her shoulder. "Everything's in here, including the garlic breadsticks from The Depot. If they would have been up front with me, I would have eaten half of them by now." Rosa had started to put some much needed weight back on her shriveled body as soon as Ricky had arrived back home. "Terry will deliver the pizzas around 7:30 like Phree asked, but I thought we could get started with a few breadsticks first."

More cars arrived, one right after the other, and the board members brought forth manila file folders, laptops, tablets, and tote bags brimming with treats. One by one all of the women got around to embracing Rosa with a welcoming hug and congratulations on her son's return. Without fail, each friend commented on how good she looked—from the fact that she had finally added a few pounds, to the fact that she looked happy. And she was. She was very happy.

"I think we've already taken care of the first order of business tonight," Phree said, "and that was to express to Rosa how thrilled we are that Ricky is home." The board members smiled and applauded softly. Rosa pressed her hands to her cheeks and closed her eyes. How thankful she was for these women. "Is there anything you'd like to tell us?" She looked at Nedra, the newly appointed secretary and said, "This is off the record, Ned."

Rosa knew that Phree had been prompted by Sunnie to ask this question. After lengthy discussions with Brian, the police, her family, and most of all Sunnie, she was prepared to share some information with her friends and ask for their confidentiality in what she was about to reveal. As Rosa disclosed the ugly and sad truth behind her son's behavior and disappearance, she became aware that except for several sharp intakes of air, sniffles, stunned faces, and head shaking, this group of usually chatty people was stunned into silence. As she struggled to tell the story, Sunnie, who was seated next to her by design, often fortified her with a light reassuring hand.

Rosa ended by looking at Sunnie and then back at the table of women. "I'm so grateful to Sunnie. Without the loving way in which she handled this situation, my son might still be on the streets frightened and alone." Having put on a brave face and telling her story with no tears, this was where Rosa broke down. Dabbing her eyes with a tissue, she continued. "You may not know this, but Sunnie visits or calls my boy every day, and he very much looks forward to spending time with her. I thank God that you took him in at City Care, and you did just that: you cared. You didn't brush him off with a single meal and send him on his way. You nurtured him and he trusted you. My family and I owe you so much, Sunnie, but all I can say is thank you…and it doesn't seem like enough."

Sunnie embraced Rosa and murmured for her ears only, "It was an honor to get to know your son. He's a very courageous boy, and my life is richer with him in it." They pulled back, still holding, and smiled at each other.

Marge, the perennial 'toaster' of the group, was the first to raise her water glass. "To Sunnie and Ricky."

Sunnie lifted her environmentally friendly water bottle and said, "And to Rosa: one brave mother who never gave up."

After a short break with hugs for both Rosa and Sunnie, and a trot to the closest Poop Deck for others, Phree resumed the meeting. "I'm going to begin with a number of small but necessary items that need to be voted on." Securing the correct page on her legal pad, she said, "First up on the agenda tonight is our ongoing discussion about Wi-Fi for the retreat goers."

Most of the women had expressed that having free Wi-Fi for the quilters would be desirable. Like it or not, it was a big part of their lives. Would quilters *not* come to the MQR if it wasn't offered? Possibly. Many people had an overwhelming need to touch base with family and work, check and send e-mails, and be able to google as desired. Nedra had pointed out, "We should encourage Facebook posts and check-ins. It's virtually free advertising for the retreat along with Twitter. I'll bet a lot of our quilters will also have quilt-related blogs that they'd update while here."

"So, unless there are any reasonable suggestions why we should *not*..." Phree made brief eye contact with each person. "I move that the Mayflower Quilters Retreat have free access to Wi-Fi for its guests."

"I second the motion."

Nedra wrote down the pertinent information.

"Next, are we all good with the last Tuesday of the month for board meetings? Any objections?" The meeting moved forward with many seemingly minor motions that needed attention, until Phree exhaled a long breath, and said, "Okay, on to meatier things."

"The Bridge, which is what we are calling the GM's office, has been finished by the contractors, electrician, painters, and everyone else involved. The various surveillance domes are installed, and the feed can be live whenever we're ready. As I'm sure you all know, Marge started last week and has things well in hand. I'm going to open the floor to our new GM, Marge Russell, and have her explain where we are in the time line and what the heck is going on around here."

Marge thumbed through some stapled papers and handed a stack to Helen who was sitting next to her. "If everyone would please take a packet and pass the rest around the table..." She launched into the details of what was happening at the retreat as far as the renovation and estimated time of completion. "It looks like we're right on track to have all construction finished by mid-September. There might be a little lag time left on finishing Phree's home, but that shouldn't have anything to do with the opening of the retreat. We're going to build in a just-in-case buffer of about three weeks, and plan for a soft opening the second week in October. This should give us enough time to deal with any unforeseen last-minute problems." Marge efficiently spelled out her first week at the MQR. She explained her excitement that she was able to secure Edyta Sitar, a favorite among quilters, as their first guest teacher for the last week of October, and the other board members nearly swooned. An unexpected cancellation had left Edyta with three available days, and Marge had snatched her up. "We'll start off the retreat with a bang by having Ms. Sitar here. I have also contacted Bonnie Hunter and Eleanor Burns, and am making a wish list of possible teachers and speakers. Let me know if you have any names or ideas that I can add."

Marge continued down her checklist and ended by saying, "The last thing I'd like to discuss is the chapel on the grounds. Phree and I have been debating what we might use the space for, and we think it would be nice as a general meeting place. All of the pews are gone, and it's basically a large, empty room which is only about fifty to sixty feet from the main building. We could put chairs up for assembly-style seating if we have a speaker or set up worktables for hands-on classes. So, for the moment, we are going to leave it empty for the purposes I've stated, but as we grow with the retreat, other needs may become obvious and necessary. Does anyone have any comments or questions?"

Sunnie signaled that she'd like to speak. "Rosa and I have been working on the quilt blocks that will act as room identifiers." This was Rosa's cue to take the small parcel from her tote bag. She handed the small package to Sunnie, who in turn offered it to Phree.

"I'm excited to see these," Phree told the group as she unwrapped white tissue paper from around the bundle. Flipping the top three over, she looked toward her mother and Rosa. "These are beautiful! I love them." As she briefly held each of the six-inch blocks up for inspection by the rest of the women around the table, Phree told the group that she would take all twenty-eight of them to the framer. "These will be so nice in addition to a boring room number. I think I want plaques for the doors that will have a numeral and then the name of the quilt block. For example, the number five with Bear's Paw beneath it or alongside of it, and then the framed Bear's Paw block will hang on the wall next to the door."

"I think our guests are going to enjoy the quilty names of their rooms more than a number," said Helen. "Not to make this an even bigger project, but what if we made wall hangings for the inside of the rooms to correspond with the names?"

"I like that," Nancy said. "In the case of the Bear's Paw room, there would be a wall hanging incorporating the Bear's Paw pattern."

"While it's a cool idea," Phree said, "that sounds like a lot of work."

"I volunteer to organize the project," Sunnie said. "Anyone interested in helping can speak to me after the meeting."

"Thanks, Sunnie. Now if there are no further comments." Phree waited a beat. "I move that we adjourn the meeting."

Rosa was glad when everyone shook their heads, and the meeting drew to an end. She knew the first several meetings would run long with all of the details of the new retreat needing to be discussed. Remembering where her head and heart were just one short month ago, she was now exceedingly happy that she had agreed to be a board member. Not only was it good for her to get out of the house, it was pretty darn exciting to be part of planning this new quilters retreat.

Alex had agreed to stay home with Ricky tonight so he wouldn't be alone. They were going to rekindle their brotherly bond by playing some video games and watching White Sox baseball at the same time. Alex had arranged the basement into a man cave for the summer with side-by-side flat screen TVs. Other than to answer the door when the pizza was delivered, they most likely wouldn't leave the basement until they went to bed.

How wonderful it was for Rosa to know that her boys were both safe at home under her roof and together again.

Chapter 33
Phree

The luxury of sleeping in was so rare, that Phree was only able to sleep twenty minutes past her usual wake-up time. Today was the Fourth of July, and there were no workers scheduled to be at the retreat. Emily would be at the pool lifeguarding all day, and then she was going to Shelley's house for a cookout. Sunnie would be attending her final July Fourth picnic with the community at City Care, where she would spend the night and drive back tomorrow morning, and Officer Bill was working a double shift for the holiday.

With slippers scuffling along the wooden floor, Phree headed toward the kitchen before showering for the day. She prepared a cup of coffee with a splash of almond syrup, and located her Kindle in a stack of unread magazines. Her e-reader had been collecting dust since she purchased the convent several months ago, and Phree planned to do a little reading before the day got away from her. She downloaded the newest book by Lisa Gardner and cozied into her favorite chair still wearing her pajamas. With time alone to read and think, she had the whole day to herself and nowhere she *had* to be. Talk about a luxury!

Lost in the latest Detective D.D. Warren story, and with her second mug of coffee recently empty, Phree clicked off the Kindle. Lounging in her pajamas had felt so good an hour ago, but now it felt just plain gross. It was time for a shower before heading to the retreat, where she planned to spend the day at the Crow's Nest. Two days ago Claire-the-designer had left three boxes of samples and a stack of brochures that Phree hadn't had a chance to look at yet. The two women had an appointment tomorrow morning to firm up her choices, so Phree thought today would be a nice, quiet time to reflect on the interior of her new home.

Typical for July in Chicagoland, it was gearing up to be a hot and steamy day. Since there was no air-conditioning in her new home at this point, Phree dressed in a sleeveless cotton shirt, a lightweight pair of capris, and flip-flops. She drew her hair into a tight ponytail, and decided at the last minute to grab a box fan from the garage. She easily could have brought the materials back here to review them in the comfortable coolness of her living room. But Phree wanted to make her choices at the Crow's Nest where the lighting was much different as it reflected off the forest surrounding her new home.

She stowed the fan and a small cooler with snacks and water in the backseat of her van. Of all the cars she could own, she was still thrilled by the fact that this vehicle was hers. It had all the bells and whistles of a luxury car, but could be the workhorse she needed in the years ahead at the retreat. As she started the car and the air kicked on, she realized that if she got too hot today, all she needed to do was sit in her car and enjoy a few minutes of cool. Her cell phone rang.

"Hello."

"We need to talk. Where are you?"

"No we don't, and that's none of your business."

"I…I just want to explain some things. It will only take five minutes."

"Gary, I'm not home. I'm taking the day off." He didn't sound drunk, but then again it was only 10:40 in the morning—give him another couple of hours and she was sure he would be over the limit. She didn't want her ex to know that she would be at the retreat, especially since she'd be alone today. "I'm spending the day in the city with Sunnie."

"I know where you were the other night."

"Huh?"

"Didn't you hear me leave my calling card?"

"I have no idea what you're talking about, nor do I care."

"I burned rubber in front of lover boy's house. You were with that gold digging son of a bitch who can only be after your money…or should I say *my* half of the money. That pompous jackass sure as hell isn't interested in a nagging bitch like you."

"Let's get something straight before I hang up on your sorry ass. You cheated on me. She got pregnant. We got divorced. You got married and now have baby number two. I owe you nothing. I can see who I please, when I please. If you'd like that in writing, I'll have my lawyer send you the memo." Phree ended the call with a smile. When her cell rang again right away, she didn't answer it.

Approaching the lane to the retreat from the main road, Phree checked for dear old Gary's car lurking in the vicinity. It appeared to be clear, so she made the turn. Holding her breath as she rounded the final curve and the retreat came into sight, she was pleased to see the parking lot was empty. Continuing around behind the Crow's Nest, instead of parking in front of the garage, she drove off the blacktop, onto the grass, and stopped her car well behind the house. There was no way her van would be visible if Gary paid an unannounced visit.

On any day but a holiday she would have notified Brian and alerted him to Gary's phone call. She toyed with letting Bill know what had happened, but she felt certain she had tricked The Bastard with her lie about being in Chicago. Just to be safe, she locked the door once she was safely inside the Crow's Nest. It was beginning to bother her a lot that she questioned his state of mind and was becoming fearful of him. One thing for sure, she wasn't going to let him ruin her peaceful day.

Phree walked between the rooms, at least the rooms where the walls were still standing, and envisioned her life here. She liked what her mind saw. It was a tranquil haven.

In the midst of the rubble from a complete makeover, Phree opened several windows, plugged in her box fan and got down to the business of decision-making. Nate had placed a six-foot, plastic-topped folding table with three folding chairs against one wall that he used as an 'office' area. In this informal space he could conference with the workers, or Claire and Phree, or other tradesman. Nudging some loose papers and a stack of blueprints to one side, she cleared a small spot and dug into Claire's box of ideas. She wanted to start with the kitchen while she was fresh; it would be the largest project on the docket today, requiring the most decisions.

She had made her selections for the appliances first. Call her old-fashioned, but she really liked the look of a crisp white stove and fridge along with a good-sized freezer. She chose a large, deep, white porcelain sink with a smaller shallow sink connected. A white microwave and dishwasher rounded out the appliance choices. She was making progress and on a roll. After much deliberation, Phree narrowed the cabinet choice to oak or cherry, and she tacked the wooden samples to the wall, while she continued debating light fixtures, the colors of too-small paint chips, and wood versus tile for the floor.

She was pleased when she checked the time and saw that it had only taken her a little over two and a half hours to nail down the perfect kitchen. Time for a break.

She stiffened her spine when she heard knocking on the back door, and Gary saying, "Open up. I know you're in there." The large bank of windows she had told Bill about the other night were not scheduled to be installed for two more weeks; otherwise, she'd be a sitting duck in here. Phree stealthily crept toward the door and loud pounding, probably with the side of his fist. "Open up. I want to talk."

"No." She answered his demand in a strong voice. "Go away, Gary. We have nothing to talk about."

"Like hell we don't. I *need* my share of the money. Why don't you just give it to me, and I'll go away."

Angry and frustrated by his annoying persistence and unreasonable belief that he was entitled to *any* of her money, tears formed in her eyes. She had long since freed herself from loving this man, but her irritation had taken on a new form—fear.

"911 what is your emergency?"

Whispering, Phree said, "I'm Phree Clarke, and I'm at the old Carmelite convent off of Monee Road inside the caretaker's cottage. My ex-husband is pounding on the door demanding that I talk to him. I have a restraining order against him."

"Is he armed?"

"I...I don't think so, but the last time he was here, he had a baseball bat."

"Stay on the line. I'm dispatching an officer."

Phree's heart matched the sound of Gary pounding on the door. And then she heard it, getting closer, a little voice that said, "Daddy, Ronny's crying."

The Bastard had his little kids with him.

"Go back to the car and shut up." He mumbled something more that Phree could not understand.

"I'm hot, and Ronny's crying."

Gary growled, "I said to shut up." He breathed heavily. "Get back in the car, Sammy."

Once you are a mother, or love a child with a mother's heart, any child in distress becomes your child. Without thinking, Phree yanked the door open and snarled, "Get those babies out of that hot car and take care of them." Somewhat surprised at what she had just done, she added, "You should be ashamed of yourself. Where's your wife?"

Gary pushed past her and went inside. At the same time Phree took advantage of the opened door and headed toward the frightened little boy. A five-year-old miniature of her ex-husband, with food stains on his clothes and two fingers stuffed in his mouth, stared wide-eyed as she approached.

"Hi, honey. I'm Emily's mom. Let's go find out what your brother is crying about."

He reached for her hand. These children were not to blame for the irresponsible way their parents had acted. They were collateral damage of an addicted gambler who had crossed paths with a young woman looking for someone to love her. They were also her daughter's half siblings, and she knew Emily loved and cared about them.

While she heard Gary cursing and sacking the inside of the Crow's Nest, she spotted the police car entering the parking lot. She was happy to see Bill was *not* in the car—that probably wouldn't have helped the situation. As the officers approached she tipped her head toward the house. "He's in there, he's been drinking, and he's pissed off. These are his kids. He left them in the car with the windows open. For their sakes, can you get him out of here without a big scene?"

One of the officers lowered his head and spoke into a microphone clipped to his collar, "We're going to need assistance. Possible child neglect. Request backup, ambulance, and DCSF worker."

"Come on, Sammy." Phree reassured the boy as they walked hand in hand to Gary's dented old car. "It's going to be okay."

Chapter 34
Rosa

The July Fourth picnic barbeque that the Mitchell family held in their backyard had been a huge success, and Rosa's surprise guest made it a perfect day. At last she felt that Ricky was on the road to a healthy recovery. She knew he still had a long way to go to reach the finish line, but watching him smiling and enjoying himself reminded Rosa of the way he was before the sad incident. As she watched her sons taking turns throwing bags, more technically called 'playing corn hole,' she once again had hope for both of their futures.

"Where's Dad?" Ricky asked. "I thought someone was covering for him at work tonight."

"I sent him to pick something up," Rosa said and flicked her eyes toward their eldest son.

Alex stood behind his brother with a large grin on his face, and placed an arm across his little brother's back. "Come on, Bro. How about a game of horse."

"I'm in."

Rosa watched carefully, so she could read the look on his face the moment he saw the surprise she had arranged with Sunnie's help. She hoped it would make him happy.

The counselor whom Sunnie had recommended was a genius as far as Rosa was concerned. Dr. Dean was working with the whole family and compassionately walking each member through their anger and grief. Ricky would have to make up his freshman year of high school and with help from Dr. Dean, they were discussing the best way to make that happen. Her son had expressed how much he regretted stealing the money and electronics from Marge's house. "It was wrong, but it was all I could figure out to do at the time," he said. "It's so much money, but somehow I want to earn enough to pay everyone back. It makes me sick what I did."

When he had confessed these thoughts to Sunnie on her first visit to see him, she said, "Let's see if we can't come up with some solutions." And in typical Sunnie form she added, "You are a good person to be so concerned about making this right."

About a week after he returned home, Rosa found him bent over at the waist crying. She laid a reassuring hand on his back and rubbed softly. "Honey, what is it?"

"I did so many mean things last year. I hate myself for being so awful to everyone." He stood and held tight to his mother, still a little boy in so many ways.

"Oh baby, with what happened we all understand."

"But that night at Marge's I know I hurt someone really bad. Someone who is nice and didn't deserve what I did to her."

Rosa knew immediately he was talking about the cruel way he had tormented Helen's red-haired daughter. She stroked his short hair, washed, cut, and smelling clean after six months on the run, and said, "Ruby Delaney."

He pulled an arm's length from her. "How did you know?"

He was correct that his comments had hurt Ruby, so she sat him down and told him the truth. The girl had been devastated when he humiliated her in front of the other teens that night. When Rosa had finished talking, Ricky said, "I feel so ashamed of myself. What should I do?"

Most of what he was going through was beyond Rosa's ability to guide him to the correct solution. "I'd say you need to apologize to her somehow. But let's talk to Dr. Dean, and even Sunnie if you want. They both seem to know how to best handle these things."

And so it went. Yes, Ricky was on the road to recovery, but he still had a very long journey ahead of him.

Before either of the boys had gotten to the letter R in horse, Ricky was executing some sort of fancy Michael Jordan spin when he stopped cold in his tracks. When he didn't move or rush forward, just stood on the driveway holding the basketball at his hip, Rosa worried that maybe she had misjudged the whole idea. Her breathing halted as Shark walked toward her son and stopped for several seconds about two feet in front of him. And then they were a tangle of arms as they gave each other a hearty man-hug and a thump or two on the other's back.

"Dude," Shark said. "I hear your name is Ricky. How ya doing, bud?"

Rosa wiped happy tears from her eyes. This boy called Shark had helped to keep her son safe for several long months.

Ricky introduced Shark to his older brother, Alex, and they shook hands. When the boys turned to Terry, Shark swatted at the air in front of him. "Pfff, Mr. M picked me up at the Metra station. We're already old friends."

The two boys walked arm in arm toward the patio where Rosa waited. "This is my mom."

"Mrs. M, good to meet you." Shark held out his hand, but Rosa ignored it, encircling the young man in a motherly hug.

"Thank you for watching out for my son. We are grateful beyond words."

"The truth is, Mrs. M, we watched out for each other. Cardo…I guess I should call him Ricky now…"

"Rick is fine. I think it sounds a little better." Ricardo Mitchell said.

Rosa glanced at Terry, eyebrows raised, as in, "Where the heck did this come from?"

"Rick and I were tight. We watched out for each other. You know he saved my life when he brought me to City Care that day?"

"He's lying. He just ate some bad food is all."

"No, Dude. You really saved my life. As in I'm living there now…roof over my head, clean clothes, my own bedroom. And I'm working there, too. Sunnie hooked me up with a permanent job before she splits to come live down here with her daughter." Shark crossed his arms over his chest. "I'm even hanging out with Megan, too."

"The Vacuum Queen?" Both boys laughed.

"The one and only. I figure the dude that marries her will have one hell of a clean house."

Rosa thought it would be nice to sometime learn this boy's real name, but right now, it was just fine to call him Shark.

Chapter 35
Phree

Two days had passed since the July Fourth fiasco with Gary. Marge sat behind her desk in the Bridge scheduling various programs and tweaking the agenda for the retreat. Nedra would show up sometime today and they would coordinate information for the social media sites they planned to set up. The new GM had supervised the installation of the phone lines and internet throughout both buildings yesterday. The head contractor suggested it was best and easiest to run the cables while the structures were torn up. It was unanimously decided that after what had happened to Phree when she was alone at the MQR, surveillance and a security system would go live sometime today.

Gary had landed his ass in jail, and Emily, like so many other kids of broken marriages or arguing parents, was hurt and confused. "I don't understand why Dad even hooked up with her in the first place," Emily said. "What did he ever see in her?"

Phree wanted to say, "Have you ever looked at her chest? That's what he saw in her." But instead she said, "I guess he saw a perky young girl who showed him attention, and at that point hadn't yet started to nag him about his bad habits. It's as simple as that, honey."

"I don't know. Tiffany's always been nice to me, but she's so young, and not to sound mean or judgmental, but she's really an airhead."

In a sort of perverse way, this made Phree happy.

"I love my little brothers though, and I feel so bad for them. What do you think will happen to Dad? And to Sammy and Ronny?"

"I don't know what Dad's going to do, but he's in a boatload of trouble." There was no use in sugarcoating what had happened. Emily would learn the truth sooner or later. "The police charged him with so many things, the least of which was tearing up our new home, that it's hard to say. Drunk driving, resisting arrest, striking an officer…and then there are the kids. Child neglect and endangerment are serious charges. The court will probably consider leaving children of that age alone in a parked car on a day when the temperatures were close to one hundred degrees a felony. When I brought Sammy back to the car, Ronny was bright red from the heat and crying."

What Phree *didn't* tell her daughter was when the EMTs arrived, little Ronny was close to passing out and they had to start an IV to get some fluids into him as fast as possible. Phree had walked a frightened Sammy toward the retreat where there was some shade, and they sat on the cool grass looking for four-leaf clovers and drinking a bottle of water the 'nice people' gave him. She hadn't wanted the little boy to see what was going on with either Ronny or his father.

"I guess Tiffany was at work," Emily said. "She's a cocktail waitress at the casino. She told me that's how she met Dad."

"No surprise there."

Emily puffed out a breath. "I'm sorry, I guess I shouldn't have said that."

"Honey, don't worry. I'm long over your father. At this point I'm actually glad I got out before it got this bad. I'm sorry for you that things didn't work out better for us as a family. It just about kills me that you've been hurt and are going to keep being hurt by your dad."

Tiffany had packed up her life and her children, and returned home to her mother. Their house was in foreclosure, and her husband was jobless and in jail. As Emily would have said, "It sucks to be her."

Sweat dripped off the tip of Phree's nose as she crossed the lawn from the Crow's Nest to the retreat. She was going to meet Nedra in about thirty minutes, and preferred to be sweat-free and stink-free by then. In the few short minutes it took to walk to the GM's office, her cotton T-shirt stuck to her back from the moisture that trickled down her spine. She had made it clear to the head contractor that they needed to have a large window air-conditioning unit temporarily installed in the Bridge as soon as the room was completed. She wanted Marge to be able to start her new career as General Manager of the Mayflower Quilters Retreat in reasonable comfort.

While Phree had willingly agreed to have another person take charge of the retreat on a full-time basis, she needed and wanted to have a daily presence there as well. At sixteen by twenty feet, the Bridge was plenty big enough to accommodate a little desk space for the owner. Phree only hoped that Marge wouldn't drive her crazy. So far, so good. She welcomed the soft hum from the window cooling unit, and dropped into her desk chair feeling hot, sticky, and sweaty.

Marge was on the phone. "Hold on please, and I'll check to see how many spots are available for the Edyta Sitar week." Phree thought Marge looked a bit frazzled. "Yes, I still have five openings. Two? Sure. I can e-mail you the forms to fill out, and as soon as I receive the payment, I'll hold the room for you." Marge looked at Phree, shrugged, and bulged her eyes open. "No, I'm sorry we're not set up for PayPal or credit cards yet, but we should be soon." Shaking her head, Marge said, "I know that won't help you now, but the good news is that everyone trying to secure a spot is in the same boat as you right now." She wrote on a notecard and read back an e-mail address to the person on the phone. "Yes, I'll send it immediately. Thank you."

Hanging up the phone, she said to Phree, "This Edyta week we have on the calendar is going crazy. I'd say you've got a big hit on your hands with this retreat, girl."

Despite the coolness from the air-conditioner, Phree fanned herself with a brochure. "Thank God. I've been worried."

"Seriously? No need for worrying." Marge kept her hands busy sorting through papers while she talked. Phree assumed she was gathering some type of in-house form for the person who had just called. "I'm glad Nedra is coming here today. We really need to get PayPal and credit card payments up on the internet as soon as possible. It has to be our number one priority."

Each woman turned her attention to waiting projects. After sending out an e-mail with the requested information, Marge started work on tweaking her filing system. While slipping manila folders into the correct order in a tall, black filing cabinet, she said, "You know, I've been thinking about what you're building here. You've put together a peaceful community for quilters and fiber artists. A place where creative people can feel safe and thrive." She stopped what she was doing and looked at Phree. "I don't know how much money you received for the documents you found," she put her hand up and shook her head, "and I don't care to know, but think about it Phree, you could have bought just about anything you ever wanted. You could move anywhere, have any size house, any type of car, but what do you do? You buy a piece of property that is one huge renovation project, with the hopes that it might someday turn into a thriving business. You buy a minivan for God's sake…a minivan! Who does *that* when they could have any model of car or cars in the world?"

Phree had to laugh. "You're not the first person to ask me that."

"I guess what I'm getting at..." Marge hesitated for a wink. "What I'm trying to say is that it's really not that much different from what your mother has dedicated her life to doing." She paused, studied the tab on a folder, and glided it to its proper alphabetic place in the file drawer. "I know you've spent a lifetime being disappointed with Sunnie, and I'm sure this is none of my business, but take it from someone whose mistakes cost her valuable time with a loved one...enjoy your mother while you still can. Think of the bigger picture."

Phree didn't respond.

Marge turned her back on Phree and carried on with filing the stack of folders, as though she had said something as unimportant as, "The bread that you like is on sale at the grocery store today."

She was initially stung by what Marge had said. *I'm just like my mother? My life's dream is basically the same as Sunnie's?* She finally found her tongue. "Do you really think we're so much alike?"

Without turning around Marge said, "Yeah, I do...two creative peas in a pod." With an exasperated sigh, Marge made eye contact with Phree. "Your mom is not here on earth solely to please you, Phree. She did the best she could, like all moms do." Further confusing Phree she said, "Do you really think that Emily hasn't found some kind of fault with the way you raised her? Wouldn't it suck if she held it against you forever?" Back to her filing, she ended her lecture to her boss by adding, "It's time to move on, girlfriend."

The meeting with Nedra turned into a working lunch. Weeks ago she had set up a blog, Twitter account, Facebook page, Linkedin, and a presence on Pinterest for the retreat. She planned to use the blog as their Web site, claiming that she felt it gave them more flexibility. "I've saved a name for a website, but we can set that up later. When we do we'll basically only use it to direct people to the blog where they will find more in-depth information." With Nedra at the helm, it didn't take long before the Mayflower Quilters Retreat blog had the capability to take payments via credit cards or PayPal.

"You're a genius," Marge told her. "This would have taken me forever, and I probably still wouldn't have done it right."

Nedra suggested that they continue to expand the 'ship theme' in their online and printed material. "Let's say something like, 'Book your passage at the Mayflower Quilters Retreat' or 'Your voyage will be from September whatever to whatever.'

"Oh! Oh!" Marge said, jittering up and down on her chair with excitement. "How about, 'Your journey will include blah, blah, blah.' "

"And when the quilters, or passengers, arrive at the retreat to start their voyage, we can greet them with, 'Welcome aboard.' "

Phree clapped her hands. "Great idea! I love it. Let's do it. Most quilters that I know are creative and like to have fun. This will spark their imagination and be right up their creative alley."

The brainstorming meeting ended when Marge's next appointment knocked on the door. She had started interviewing for housekeepers, an executive chef, and three people to form the maintenance crew. Marge would narrow down the prospects, and then along with Phree, they would make the final decision together.

Leaving the office and entering the heat of a July afternoon, Nedra said to Phree, "If you have a minute, I've got some sketches of the Mayflower quilt I've been thinking about."

"Let's head over to the Crow's Nest. I'd like to show you what's going on there, too." Without a doubt, Nedra was the fashionista of the eight good friends, and Phree was thankful when she saw that her friend had worn flat shoes today. "We'll cut across the grass. It'll be quicker. At some point there will be a sidewalk here, so a safe path can be shoveled in the wintertime."

"You've thought of everything. I'm impressed with all of the planning that you've done."

"Thanks for the compliment, but I have a team of professionals who come up with most of the ideas and are guiding me through the process."

Walking around the back of her new home to what Phree was calling the forest entrance, she saw a crew of workers setting in the massive wall of windows.

"Holy crap," said Nedra. "This is going to be stunning."

"Come on in, I'll show you around."

They entered through the same door through which Gary had pushed past her two days ago. "A very cool set of French doors will replace this entryway." Phree spotted Nate, head bent over some blueprints at the contractor's table, writing notes on a piece of paper. "I want to introduce you to someone. Follow me."

Phree intentionally blocked Nedra's view of the man spearheading the renovation of the Crow's Nest. If she had told Nedra, "There's this hot-looking available middle-aged black man I want you to meet," her friend would have bolted in the opposite direction. "Hi Nate. How's it going today?"

Handsome Nate smiled as Phree approached, unaware that a second person was weaving her way through the detritus of the construction site behind his client. "We're making good progress. Those windows should be in by..." Nedra stepped from behind Phree, and Nate stopped talking for a moment. "...ah, by...ah, tomorrow at this time." He gained composure and his eyes popped back into his head.

"Great. They're every bit as beautiful as Clair said they'd be." Phree looked at Nedra as though she were surprised to see anyone standing beside her. "Oh, this is my friend Nedra Lange. Nedra, this is Nate Williams. Nate and his son Josh are the chief visionaries behind everything that's going on here."

After swiping his right hand on the side of his jeans, he offered it to Nedra and said, "Nice to meet you, ma'am."

"Likewise, but please, call me Nedra."

Phree noticed that their eyes locked onto each other, and the friendly handshake lasted a little longer than necessary. She smiled as it occurred to her that she just might have some talents when it came to matchmaking.

Sunnie walked through the door and joined the small group. "Those windows are breathtaking, Nate. Good job convincing my daughter she should have them."

Phree said, "It didn't take much convincing."

"Can I borrow you for a minute, Phree? I'm sorry, Nate. I'll bring her right back."

"No problem." He turned to Nedra. "Would you like a virtual tour of the building site? Have a seat." He pulled out one of the folding chairs and 'Miss Priss' took a seat in the midst of the chaos of construction grunge.

Sunnie led her daughter through the door and outside.

"Perfect timing," Phree said. "I'll give them about twenty minutes to get acquainted." The two conspirators giggled, and walked toward the quilters retreat together.

Chapter 36
July Bunco at Phree's

The beauty of having her ex-husband rotting in jail was that Phree no longer had to worry about him physically hurting their daughter. Emily would be leaving for the University of Iowa in three and a half short weeks. The campus was just far enough away for a college freshman to feel as though she was on her own, but still close enough if either mom or daughter felt the need to connect. How the heck had her daughter grown so fast?

"Did they have that gluten-free cake mix?" Phree asked as Sunnie came into the kitchen carrying a reusable cloth tote that she always used when grocery shopping.

"Yep. I also picked up some gluten-free crackers, a dozen eggs, and an extra-large bag of ice."

"Smart thinking on the ice." Phree was hosting the Bunco group tonight, and both she and Sunnie were playing hooky from their duties at the retreat today. They'd be working side by side to spruce up the house and get the rest of the food prepared. "I hope we don't discover anything else I forgot to get at the store yesterday."

"Where would you like me to start?" Sunnie asked.

"The three hot spots are the family room, the kitchen, and the bathroom. No one ever goes any farther down the hall than that, so we don't have to worry about the rest of the house." Phree finger combed her hair into a ponytail and using a clip snapped the wayward tendrils into place. "Your choice. I'll do whatever you don't want to."

"Let's flip for it."

"You're kidding."

"No, I'm not. Dad and I always used to flip for unpleasant jobs."

Phree scoffed. "I never saw you two flip for a job…or anything for that matter."

"There's a lot of things you never saw us do, but that doesn't mean we didn't do them."

By this time Sunnie had slipped her hand into her front pocket and had a quarter balancing on her sideways fisted hand. "Call it. Loser gets the bathroom."

Before Phree could think, Sunnie sent the coin spinning through the air, and Phree shouted, "Heads!" The quarter pinged as it hit the wooden floor and traveled a wobbly eight to nine feet in a big semicircular arc. Sunnie shrieked and chased after the rolling currency, elbowing to get in front of her daughter. Slowing from a frenetic spin to an unsteady tilt, the quarter finally landed flat on the floor.

"Crap!" Sunnie wailed, and then, dead serious, said, "Two out of three?"

Laughing, Phree fanned her premenopausal flushed face. "I don't think I could do that two more times."

"Party poop."

"Tell you what," Phree told her mom. "I'll take the bathroom, and you start in the family room."

"Deal."

At nearly sixty years old, Sunnie punched her hand toward Phree for a fist bump.

Lemony scents wove through the pungent chemical odors from an army of cleaning supplies. Sunnie was still spritzing, vacuuming, dusting, and sneezing her way to a clean family room, when Phree stopped at the double door to tell her mother she was going to start work in the kitchen.

"I'm almost done. Be there shortly," Sunnie answered.

Tapping her finger on the menu that she and Sunnie had created a few days ago, Phree mentally checked off the items that had already been prepared. All that was left to make was the gluten-free cake and frosting for Lettie (who had recently been diagnosed as gluten sensitive), assembling a fruit and cheese tray, and making freshly popped popcorn. Then they could perform a quick clean up on the kitchen, take showers, set up the Bunco tables and supplies, and put out the food. Phree was thankful her mother was there to help.

Sunnie entered the kitchen and puffed out a breath. "Now what?" She retrieved a cold bottle of water from the fridge and swiped it across her cheeks a few times before resting it on her forehead. "Ah, that feels better." Leaning against the counter, she took a long draft of the chilled water.

"All I can say is, thank God for disposable plastic gloves," Phree said. "With spending so much time at the retreat, I'm embarrassed at how long it's been since that bathroom's been swabbed down. I have officially decided that when I finally move to the Crow's Nest, I'm going to hire a cleaning lady."

"Good for you. You deserve to pamper yourself a little. It'll free up more time for quilting."

"Hear, hear." Phree raised her frosty, sweating water bottle for a toast and then took a long swig of the icy liquid. She thoughtfully twisted the cap back on and said, "You've been a big help. I'm happy you're here."

"My pleasure, missy." Sunnie passed her daughter on the way to the cabinet that housed the electric hand mixer and rested her hand on Phree's shoulder for a beat. "I'm having a ball hanging out with you and Emily."

The mixer whirred the gluten-free cake mix into a creamy batter, while Phree assembled a lineup of fruits on the counter to be sliced, chopped, and cut into bite-size pieces. Sunnie clicked off the mixer and using a bowl scraper deposited every last drop of the chocolaty blend into a cake pan. Phree thought this might be a good time to share something that had begun to tickle the edges of her brain.

"After Emily is away at college, I think I'm going to change my name." Continuing to quarter the basket of strawberries in front of her, Phree kept her eyes down. "What do you think?"

Sunnie glided the cake pan onto the rack of the preheated oven, closed the door, and left the kitchen without saying a word. Phree gave her mom a few minutes—maybe she had to use the washroom...the very *clean* washroom. When Sunnie hadn't appeared by the time all the berries had been sliced, Phree rinsed the stickiness from her hands and went to look for her.

Sunnie stood with her arms crossed over her chest, gazing out of the picture window, rubbing warmth into her chilled limbs.

"Are you okay?"

Nodding her head, Sunnie croaked out, "Yeah, I'm fine."

Phree heard the distress in her mother's voice and placed a hand on her back. "No, you're not fine. What's wrong?"

Swatting at the air in front of her face with both hands, Sunnie brushed off the question. "Nothing really. I just had a moment."

"Don't give me that nothing's wrong crap. Come on. Let's sit down and talk about it." Phree knew that her mother rarely had 'moments.' That was a big reason why Wolf had given her the name Sunshine—as in 'she's always positive and brightens one's life. Only days after their marriage ceremony, they both legally changed their names, and Audrey Christine Piekarski had become Sunshine Eaton. "What gives?"

At the end of a long exhale, Sunnie said one word. "Regret."

Phree cocked her head to one side. "What do you mean?"

"One of my many regrets is that we saddled you with such a weird name. I'm sorry, honey. I know how much you hate it. If you want to change it, I understand—I really do. I just don't want this to get in the way of our relationship…our new friendship."

Phree chuckled. "No, no, no. I love my name. People never forget it." Sunnie looked confused, and Phree continued, "I was eight when I said I hated my name. Bobby McCormick used to call me Ding-dong, because he said I was named after the Liberty Bell."

"But you just said you were thinking of changing your name."

"Clarke. I don't want to be Phree *Clarke* anymore. Gary's a creep headed straight for jail, and Emily is old enough not to feel awkward if I suddenly have a different last name. I want to change it back to Eaton. Phreedom Eaton."

Sunnie smiled. "I like that."

"So, the soon to be Ms. Phreedom Eaton has a regret of her own she'd like to discuss."

"…And?"

"Well," Phree rubbed a strawberry stain on the bottom of her T-shirt. "I'm sorry that I've been such an ass…a self-centered adult ass, which might just be the worst kind. I've been acting like a spoiled little kid for years, and I'm sorry."

"Apology accepted."

"I started to see you in a different light when the whole Ricky Mitchell thing blew up. You were amazing. When you left for a few days to help someone that I loved and cared about, I didn't mind at all. Then I realized all of the people that you have helped over the years…well, they all had someone who loved and cared about them, too. It occurred to me that none of my griping was called for. Maybe I simply threw myself a twenty-year pity party. Maybe I wasn't being fair. Maybe I was jealous and wanted you all to myself. Maybe it was all of the above. So, again, I'm sorry." And then she added, "Mom."

Phree could see that Sunnie was trying to hold back from crying—Ms. Sunshine did *not* cry. But when one tear escaped the red-rimmed barricade of her eyelids, there was nothing she could do to stop their flow. "Yes. Let's start over."

Phree was determined to be at peace with her mother, resolute to overlook quirks that had always annoyed her, while remembering the wisdom that Marge had shared: *It's time to let go.* She would try. Old habits *did* die hard, as the saying went, but Phreedom Aquarius Eaton Clarke Eaton was about to become best friends with her mother—even if it nearly killed both of them.

With her eyes toward the clock and her mind focused on how little time was left before the Bunco Club arrived, Phree stood, held out her hand to her mother, and said, "Shall we?"

But Sunnie tugged on her hand to sit. "There's one more thing I'd like to discuss." Phree sat down when she heard the serious tone in her mother's voice. "This decision will be entirely up to you. No questions asked and no hard feelings."

"Go ahead."

"Is there any way that we can give Ricky a part-time job at the retreat? He is desperate to pay the money and items back that he stole last year from Marge's house. He's a good kid, Phree. I think he'd be good at—"

Phree held both of her hands up for Sunnie to stop talking. She looked at her mother over the top of her cheater glasses while shaking her head. Phree saw her mother brace herself for a rebuff, and waited a wink to reply. "Don't say anything more. Absolutely, one hundred percent, yes. He can start whenever he feels ready. There's plenty of work at the retreat that could be done by an able-bodied and willing fifteen-year-old boy. Helping Ricky Mitchell will be good for everyone concerned."

Sunnie's smile was brightest when she was helping someone, and Phree felt her chest swell with pride that she was this wonderful woman's daughter.

By 7:30 all the Bunco girls had arrived for food and a fun-filled night of Bunco. Due to the heat and humidity, it was unanimously agreed that there would be *no* outdoor activities tonight. "Even eating makes me sweat," Rosa said. Plates were piled high with the delicacies that Phree and Sunnie had prepared, and chilled white wine splashed liberally into long-stemmed wineglasses.

"Okay, ladies, I've got a little surprise slash gossip for you," Nedra said. "Actually, two." The room became as hushed as a confessional on Saturday afternoon, as the women's full attention shifted toward Nedra. "Where to start?" She pondered by drumming her fingertips on her lips and looking skyward.

"With the juiciest tidbit first," Rosa said.

"In that case," Nedra paused for dramatic effect. "I had a date."

Screams and hoots filled the room. Marge let loose with one of her two-fingered wolf whistles.

"Spill," Lettie commanded.

"Who?" said Nancy.

"That gorgeous contractor who's working at the retreat." Phree and Sunnie knew about this little morsel of information from Nate, but had agreed they would keep it hush-hush until Nedra decided to talk about it. "He took me out for dinner, and I actually had a wonderful time. I hate to say it, and I'd never tell Nate, but he reminds me a little of John. He's smart and respectful and is a great talker. I like him."

"We'll be talking more about this later," said Beth. "But I want to know what your second bombshell is?"

"All right ladies, this might even be harder to believe than the fact that I've got a love life."

"Holy crap." Helen grabbed the wine bottle and held it up. "Who needs more?"

"Seriously, I'm glad we're all sitting," Nedra said. "Starting in September, after my girls go back to college, I'm taking an extended leave of absence from *Excel.*"

"No way!"

"You?"

"What the heck," Rosa said. "Why?"

Nedra sipped some wine and placed a handful of chocolate-covered raisins on her empty plate. "After I wrote the Mayflower article for *Excel* I got to thinking. My girls are in college, I'm not getting any younger, and I still want to write a book or preferably books." Shaking a pointer finger at Marge, she said, "You inspired me. If you can leave your job for something you love…for a dream, why shouldn't I?"

"I agree," said Lettie. "I suppose we all agree." Every member of the Bunco group nodded her head.

"Like Marge said before, it's for my psyche and the spirit in me."

"And my soul is already full to bursting," Marge told everyone. "It was a smart move on my part. Smart, but very scary. How's this all going to work, Ned? Do you have a strategy in place?"

"I plan on getting up every day at the same time I do now and writing until about one in the afternoon," Nedra said. "That'll be about seven hours. If I want to write longer, I will…if not, I'll head over to the retreat and work on our social media sites and various brochures or anything else that needs to be done."

"Any idea what subject your books will be about?" Phree asked.

"Well…maybe I've got an idea or two. I'm thinking about two completely different scenarios."

"Can you share?" Helen asked.

"I'd like to write an historical fiction novel about the women of the Mayflower. I've been so amped up after doing research and writing the piece for *Excel.* I can't get that tattered group of people and their struggles out of my mind."

"You said two scenarios. What's the other one?" Rosa said.

"Well, this idea is more personal. I'm toying with a story about a group of friends who play Bunco every month. I want to base it on the friendship within our own group," she held up her hand, "but don't worry, none of our stories will find their way into my book. Your secrets are safe with me. It'll be all fiction."

"Those are both very cool ideas, Ned. I can't wait to read what you come up with."

Nedra laughed, "Neither can I."

The eight friends drifted into separate conversations and soon after began to play Bunco. Sunnie bustled about the room gathering up used plates and any other rubbish that was lying around. She would sit in at either table and sub if someone needed a potty break, or top off wineglasses and candy dishes that might need refilling. By the time the game was over and Marge was tallying up the scores, Sunnie had the family room and kitchen cleaned up and a hot pot of tea with the desserts resting on the table.

As the women seated themselves at the dining room table for the various sweets that they would enjoy, Phree walked up to her mother and slipped an arm around Sunnie's thin waist. The past several months had allowed her to grow close to her mother. Taking responsibility for being an unreasonable daughter and following Marge's advice had liberated her to appreciate and love this woman more than she would have ever dreamed possible. "How about a round of applause for my amazing mother and all of the help she gave us tonight?"

"You don't have to ask me twice," Rosa shouted over the clapping. "The Mitchells are already lifetime members of the 'Sunnie Eaton Fan Club.' "

Sunnie appeared to be embarrassed, but Phree had one more thing she wanted everyone to know. "You can call us the Eaton girls from now on," she said, tugging her mother's waist close to her own. "I'll soon be Phreedom Aquarius Eaton again. I'm kicking The Bastard to the curb for the last time and taking back the wonderful name that my mother and father gave me when I was born."

As usual, it was Marge who proposed a toast. The table of close friends all raised their empty teacups as Marge said, "Long live the Eaton girls. And long live the Mayflower Quilters Retreat."

Karen is available for quilt guild talks, library talks, and book club discussions. Contact her at KarenDeWitt7@gmail.com or by visiting her blog at **KarenDeWittAuthor.blogspot.com.**

Karen DeWitt is an avid quilter who holds an MFA in studio art. She is also a member of a Bunco Club that has been together for more than twenty years. Karen lives in the Chicago suburbs with her husband, and they have one adult son.